LEGENDS

TALES FROM THE DANE MADDOCK UNIVERSE

DAVID WOOD

ADRENALINE PRESS

"Classic adventure for the modern reader!"

A vanished island of horrors.
An ancient artifact that can change the course of the past.
An urban legend come to life.
A perilous expedition into the jungle.
A dangerous game where the stakes are life and death.

LEGENDS is a collection of four short stories and a novella from the Dane Maddock universe. It includes URBAN LEGEND, AZTLAN, PHANTOM ISLAND, DARK ENTRY, and VENOM!

"David Wood has done it again. Within seconds of opening the book, I was hooked. Intrigue, suspense, monsters, and treasure hunters. What more could you want? David's knocked it out of the park with this one!" Nick Thacker- author of *The Enigma Strain*

"A twisty tale of adventure and intrigue that never lets up and never lets go!" Robert Masello, author of *The Einstein Prophecy*

"A page-turning yarn blending high action, Biblical speculation, ancient secrets, and nasty creatures. Indiana Jones better watch his back!" Jeremy Robinson, author of *SecondWorld*

"With the thoroughly enjoyable way Mr. Wood has mixed speculative history with our modern day pursuit of truth, he has created a story that thrills and makes one think beyond the boundaries of mere fiction and enter the world of 'why not'?" David Lynn Golemon, Author of the *Event Group* series

"Let there be no confusion: David Wood is the next Clive Cussler. Once you start reading, you won't be able to stop until the last mystery plays out in the final line." Edward G. Talbot, author of *2012: The Fifth World*

"I like my thrillers with lots of explosions, global locations and a mystery where I learn something new. Wood delivers! Recommended as a fast paced, kick ass read." J.F. Penn, author of *Desecration*

Legends- ©2020 by David Wood

The Dane Maddock Adventures™

All rights reserved

Published by Adrenaline Press
www.adrenaline.press

Adrenaline Press is an imprint of Gryphonwood Press
www.gryphonwoodpress.com

ISBN: 978-1-950920-18-1

BOOKS BY DAVID WOOD

Herald
Brainwash
The Tomb
Shasta
Legends
Destination: Rio
Destination: Luxor
Destination: Sofia

JADE IHARA ADVENTURES (WITH SEAN ELLIS)
Oracle
Changeling
Exile

MYRMIDON FILES (WITH SEAN ELLIS)
Destiny
Mystic

BONES BONEBRAKE ADVENTURES
Primitive
The Book of Bones
Skin and Bones
Lost City

JAKE CROWLEY ADVENTURES (WITH ALAN BAXTER)
Sanctum
Blood Codex
Anubis Key
Revenant

BROCK STONE ADVENTURES
Arena of Souls
Track of the Beast (forthcoming)

SAM ASTON INVESTIGATIONS (WITH ALAN BAXTER)
Primordial
Overlord

STAND-ALONE NOVELS
Into the Woods (with David S. Wood)
The Zombie-Driven Life
You Suck
Callsign: Queen (with Jeremy Robinson)
Dark Rite (with Alan Baxter)

WRITING AS FINN GRAY
Aquaria Falling
Aquaria Burning
The Gate

WRITING AS DAVID DEBORD

THE ABSENT GODS TRILOGY
The Silver Serpent
Keeper of the Mists
The Gates of Iron

The Impostor Prince (with Ryan A. Span)
Neptune's Key

CONTENTS

FROM THE AUTHOR

This collection includes four previously published short stories and one novella that was briefly published as part of the Kindle Worlds program. The novella, VENOM, is a shorter, lighter treatment of the Yacumama legend that served as the inspiration for the novel SERPENT. I am including it in this collection because many readers have expressed interest in reading it.

"Phantom Island" was originally published in the Severed Press anthology PREHISTORIC under the title "Lost Island." It has been rewritten to make it a part of the Maddock universe.

"Dark Entry" was originally published as a short story, then rewritten and incorporated into the novel, ARK. It appears here in its original form.

"Aztlan" and "Urban Legend" have been published individually and as bonus stories in other Maddock works.

Thank you for reading "Legends." I hope you enjoy it!

David

URBAN LEGEND

Urban Legend: (noun) A horrific story or piece of information circulated as though it was true.

When Willis Sanders is called upon to locate a missing person, he comes face to face with a real-life urban legend...but can he escape with his life?

This short story originally appeared as a bonus story in *The Dane Maddock Adventures: Volume 2.*

URBAN LEGEND

Willis Sanders pulled his RAV 4 into the abandoned parking lot, stopped, and cut the engine. The headlights faded away, leaving only the faint gray glow of the cloud-covered moon to illuminate their surroundings. Knee-high weeds encircled the cracked asphalt square. Twenty yards away, a sparse tree line barred the way to their destination.

"You're trying to tell me this is where my cousin is staying?"

"I don't know that he lives here, but I'm sure he *was* here," said Zoe. "And he didn't look like he was going anywhere any time soon."

"Man, I still can't believe I let my Mama talk me into this. Lonzo ain't never been no good. Even if I find him, he ain't going to want to go with me. Probably have to knock him out and carry him away." The former Navy SEAL, now a professional treasure hunter, had come home to Detroit to visit family. He hadn't been home twenty-four hours before his mother and his aunt had guilt tripped him into finding his wayward cousin, who hadn't been home in several days.

"So, don't go." Zoe turned to face him, intensity flaring in her rheumy eyes. "I'm not kidding, Willis, it's a crazy ass place. All them urban legends about this place have to come from somewhere." A spasm of coughs, wet and phlegmy, racked her chest. She opened the door and spat on the ground.

"Urban legends come from superstitious people and folks with too much imagination." Willis, still weary from the drive up from Key West, Florida, rubbed his eyes and yawned.

Zoe shook her head. "You better be on your toes if you're going in there."

"Girl, I promise you I've seen more dangerous places than an abandoned mental hospital. Now, tell me where you saw Lonzo."

Zoe raised her eyebrows. "You're not leaving me here alone. I'd rather be with you in there," she pointed toward the trees, "than out here by myself. I don't like being anywhere near this place."

Willis heaved a heavy sigh. He and Zoe had been friends since junior high, and he knew from long experience there was no point in arguing with her. "All right. Come on, then."

They picked their way through the overgrown landscaping, careful not to step on the broken glass, old syringes, and occasional mounds of human waste. As the dark, hulking outlines of several buildings came into view, he spotted a faded sign, its paint peeling.

Northville Psychiatric Hospital.

"I think a couple of my exes probably spent a little time here." He cast a sideways glance at Zoe, whose expression didn't change. He'd noticed a dramatic difference in her since he'd picked her up an hour before.

Zoe, even during the lowest times in her life, had always been upbeat and positive. Now she seemed sullen, preoccupied, even a little twitchy. Her cheeks were drawn, her full lips were tight, thin lines.

"What can you tell me about this place?" he asked.

"Northville Psychiatric. It started out all right. The doctors here were pioneers in art and music therapy. They took care of the patients. Then, back in the seventies, the state cut back the budget for mental health care and things got bad. Overcrowded, understaffed, the hospital used heavy medication instead of intense therapy. Pretty soon, they couldn't afford to hire good people, didn't always have beds for all the patients."

Willis nodded, remembering the story. Investigative reporters in the early eighties discovered patients spending their days smoking and watching television, fighting with the staff and with one another. At night, many slept in the hallways. Assault, rape, and unexplained deaths were commonplace. Minority patients got the worst of it at the hands of prejudiced staff. He was surprised he'd forgotten such an ugly story.

"They finally shut the place down about fifteen years ago," Zoe said. "They say some of the residents never left."

Ordinarily, Willis would have chuckled at this proclamation, but Zoe's serious expression and deadpan tone silenced him. What she was saying might be a pile of crap, but she believed it.

"The city discourages people from coming here. They say it's for our safety, talk about asbestos and crumbling buildings." Zoe paused. "But the thing is, even though they're so concerned, the police never patrol here. If you come here then post a pic or video on social media, they'll come after you. But they won't go in, won't even drive onto the property."

"So, I won't find a parking ticket on my windshield when we get back?"

Zoe shook her head. "And don't bother calling 911. They won't send anybody out here." She took a deep breath. "It started with rumors of strange noises, screams, moans. Then people started reporting ghost sightings. And recently, folks who have gone in here have come back all crazy in the head." She lowered her voice to a whisper.

"Or they don't come back at all."

"That ain't exactly unusual for old places, especially places like this."

Willis cocked his head. "So why did you come out here?"

She made a face. "There are twenty buildings. Not all of them are dangerous."

Up ahead loomed a nine-story brick building. Moonlight gleamed off its rows of dirty windows. His eyes roved along the contours, taking in the sagging roof, broken glass, and down to the crumbling steps. The sight sent a chill down his spine. Generally speaking, he wasn't a big believer in urban legends, but he'd seen enough crazy stuff in his time to know improbable did not equal impossible.

"Not that one," Zoe said. "We don't want to go in there."

"Is that where the ghosts are?"

"Don't be an ass. I don't care if you believe me or not. This place isn't right."

"Come on, girl. I'm just asking." He reached out and took her hand.

"It's not fair, you know," she said, looking up at him.

"What's that?"

"You're so dark, you blend right in. I'm lighter than you. The ghosts will see me first." She forced a smile.

Willis put his arm around her shoulders. "Don't worry. I got you. Which building is it?"

Zoe pointed. "It's over that way."

Zoe froze, pointed a trembling finger. "What is that?"

Up ahead, an eerie glow turned the fog a faint, flickering yellow. In its midst rose a dark figure. Willis pushed Zoe behind him. The figure grew in stature, elongated, growing impossibly thin. Willis relaxed.

"Somebody's got a fire going up there. We're just seeing a shadow in the fog."

Moving on silent feet, he crept up until he saw a man bundled up in several layers of ragged clothing, hunched over a tiny fire. He was roasting a rat on a stick. Seeing no need to disturb the urban camper, Willis held a finger to his lips to indicate Zoe should remain silent as they crept along outside the ring of light.

"That was nasty," Zoe said when they were out of earshot.

"I've eaten worse." He'd been in numerous survival situations that required him to eat whatever he could scavenge. He definitely preferred a barbecue, but not when rat was on the menu.

Zoe stopped short and pressed her hand to her forehead.

"What's up?"

"Nothing." She squeezed her eyes tightly shut and slowly shook her head. "I've had a migraine for a couple of days. Ever since… never mind. Let's hurry this up."

"Fine by me," Willis said. "Are we close?"

Zoe scanned the surrounding buildings. "I'm not sure."

"What do you mean? Weren't you just here?"

"I was in a hurry to leave. Come on, I think it's this way." She took him by the hand and led him toward a low, single-story building. The door stood ajar, inky blackness beyond.

Zoe was whispering to herself. "Yeah, I remember. It's down. Way down."

The door was jammed but Willis had no trouble forcing it. They stepped into a narrow corridor, the floor cracked and covered with debris. To the left, dirty windows permitted enough light to reveal a row of doors, all painted green, along the right wall. The dank smell of stale water filled the space.

"You got a flashlight?" Zoe asked.

"Yeah, but we don't need it just yet. Which way do we go?"

Zoe bit her lip, and then strode down the corridor, trying each door. The third door opened on what had once been an office. Willis could make out the shape of a broken-down desk and a smashed computer monitor. Old, waterlogged newspapers covered the floor. As his eyes took in the details of the small room, he spotted writing on the wall to his right. His night vision was good, though no match for his friends Maddock and Bones, but before he could read the words, a blinding light flared in front of him.

"Forgot my phone had a flashlight on it," Zoe said. She raised the light and let out a tiny gasp as she read the words spray painted on the wall in scarlet.

YOU WON'T MAKE IT OUT ALIVE

She turned to Willis. "I think we should go back."

He shook his head. "Not until we find Lonzo, or I decide he can't be found. Now, turn that thing off before somebody sees."

Zoe immediately snapped off the light, plunging them into darkness. As they stood, waiting for their eyes to adjust, Willis felt her give his hand a squeeze.

"I'm not sure I can find the place again," Zoe said, voice trembling. "I'm sure Lonzo is long gone by now."

Willis seized her by the shoulders. "Girl, I need you to stop messing around. Why did you come here in the first place, and don't lie."

He felt her shoulders sag as the tension drained from her body. Slowly, she sank to the floor and buried her face in her hands.

"I was making a run for a dude named Lance." Her voice was muffled.

"A run? Damn, Zoe, I thought you left all that behind."

She lifted her chin and stared at him, her face just visible. "You don't know what it's like. You were born here, but you aren't from here, not any more. Some of us got to do whatever we can to get by."

"I hear you." Her words stung, but it was true. Whenever he came back to visit his family, he didn't truly feel like he was home. Sometimes it felt like his life began in the Navy, and his life before that was a faded dream. "Who is this Lance? He don't sound like he's from around here either."

"White dude. He's new but he's already big-time. Well, he's getting there, anyway. He pays good and he's the only one dealing plant."

Willis scratched his head. "Weed?"

"No, they just call it plant. It's different. Anyway, he's got people growing it here, but he needed locals to carry it—people who won't stand out. He got my name from Lonzo, who's been working for him, and the money was good."

"Why can't his people deliver it? White folks ain't exactly unicorns."

At his words, Zoe pressed her hand to her forehead. Realizing what she'd done, she pulled it away quickly. "Sorry. Head still hurting." She took a breath. "It wouldn't work for his people to deliver. I can't explain it."

"All right. So you do know where we need to go?"

"Yes, but I don't want to go back there. I can't."

Willis sighed and sat down cross-legged in front of her. Despite his rising impatience, he tried to adopt a soothing manner. "Tell me everything you can. What do they have here? A greenhouse? A lab?"

"They're growing stuff here, but I wouldn't call it a greenhouse." Zoe's voice took on a forbidding tone.

"Is Lonzo carrying, like you, or is he involved in the growing"

"He's growing," Zoe snapped. Her face had gone ashen, her eyes wide.

"Did you see the plants?"

"It's one big plant. They grow it underground in a room full of red lights. There's a big dome up above it, like they want to keep the water off. This whole complex was a marsh once, and water drips everywhere. Maybe the ground water's too polluted. Anyway, they take this one part of the plant and, when they finish with it in the lab, it comes out as a fine, reddish brown powder. Almost looks like dried blood."

"Do they snort it? Mix it up in water and drink it?"

"You can't drink it. Water makes it lose all its potency. They must have told me ten times how important it was that I keep it dry."

Willis ran a hand over his shaved scalp. "What does the drug do?"

"I haven't tried it." Zoe didn't quite manage to meet Willis' eye as she spoke. "But they say it makes you think you're lots of other people. You jump through flashes of their lives like flipping through the channels on a TV."

Willis thought that sounded unsettling and not at all what one would want from a recreational drug. "What about Lonzo? You said he's helping with the growing. Is he safe? I mean, as safe as someone working with drug dealers can be. Do you think he's free to leave if he wants?"

Zoe let out a pained moan and covered her face again. "I don't think he can leave, and even if you could get to him, there's nothing you could do about it."

"He hasn't been gone too long. How could he already be in that deep?"

Zoe gazed at the open window, tears streaming down her face. "It can happen fast."

"I've got to at least check it out for myself. You don't have to come if you don't want to. You can hide here until I come back."

"No. I need to go."

Willis quirked an eyebrow. "Just like that?"

"I don't want to go, but it's important." She stood and headed for the doorway. "You get in through the steam tunnels, but a lot of them are collapsed. The way in is through the bowling alley. Come on."

Willis was surprised to learn that, among its many amenities, Northville had its own bowling alley. They crept through the dark, swampy campus, the air foul with stagnant water, until they reached their destination. He knew immediately that something was wrong.

"Voices," he whispered. "Somebody's inside. You think it's some of the dealer's people?"

"I doubt it," Zoe said. "The plant and the lab are still a long way from here. Besides, they're discreet."

Willis moved to a cracked window and peered inside. Someone had hung black fabric over it, but through a narrow gap on the edge, he could see inside. Propane lanterns set at regular intervals shone white circles of light out onto the bowling lanes. The wood hadn't been waxed or tended to in many years, and it lacked the usual shine.

To the left, at the head of the nearest lane, three men stood drinking beer, talking and laughing loudly. All were pasty white with shaved heads. They wore sleeveless shirts, revealing a variety of tattoos: swastikas, Confederate flags, skulls with the word 'skins' inside them, and clenched white fists surrounded by laurels.

"White power my ass," Willis whispered.

As he watched, one of the skinheads hefted a bowling ball and flung it carelessly down the lane. Willis followed its trajectory and his eyes fell on what he hadn't seen before. A young black man, bound and gagged, sat where the pins should be. His ankles were secured wide apart, providing a painful target for a well-placed throw. As he watched, the ball struck the young man on the inner calf and rebounded over to the opposite leg. Willis couldn't hear the youth's angry cry, but he saw the way his eyes bulged, his neck strained as he twisted within his bonds.

"Goddamn skinheads." He looked back at the laughing men. None of them appeared to be armed. "We gonna see about this."

"Oh, you think so?"

Willis turned to see a fourth skinhead standing a few paces away. He was holding Zoe tight against him, his left hand covering her mouth. In his right hand he held a pistol pressed against her temple.

"You must be the hooker delivery service," the skinhead said. "She's a nice one, but I think she might be infected with something. Bitch is burning up."

Still crouched by the window, Willis quickly assessed the situation. The man had his finger on the trigger. He was just far enough away that he would almost certainly get a shot off if Willis were to make a move. He needed to get closer.

"Come on, man," he said, raising his hands, "we're just checking the place out. We ain't got no beef with you."

The man grinned. "I got some beef for your girl here." He jerked her head around, leaned in, and planted a kiss on her lips. In doing so, he pulled the gun away from her head.

That was all the opening Willis needed. He sprang forward, his fist connecting with the skinhead's jaw just to the left of the chin. As the man's knees wobbled, Willis tore the pistol from his grasp.

The skinhead recovered surprisingly quickly. He wobbled back a few steps and drew a knife.

"You don't have the guts, boy," he said, flashing a crooked, yellow smile. "Not just anybody can point a gun at a man and pull the trigger. And even less can hit a moving target. You ever killed a man? I mean, a real man. Not one of your ghetto…"

His words died in a ragged gurgle as Willis' first shot tore through his throat. The second bullet made him a eunuch. Willis pulled the trigger again, but the magazine was empty. "Two damn bullets? Broke ass son of a bitch."

Zoe pressed her fingers to her lips, her eyes wide.

"Sorry you had to see that," Willis said, staring down at the dying man.

"I've seen plenty of people killed before," she said. "I just can't believe how good you can shoot."

"You think that's good, you ought to see my friend, Maddock. Dude don't miss." Willis took a few seconds to wipe the pistol clean, then tuck it into his pocket. He had a plan.

Inside the bowling alley, the three remaining skinheads were still drinking. Their captive sat forgotten at the end of the lane. Willis watched them for a long time, trying to determine if they were armed. He saw no weapons, but had to assume they at least had knives. They did not appear to be on alert. The pop of the small caliber pistol must not have reached this far. Or, maybe the sound of gunfire wasn't all that unusual here.

Zoe had told him the way down into the blocked steam tunnel was directly behind where the captive young man now sat. Even if that had not been the case, Willis wouldn't have left him behind except in the direst of circumstances. Besides, he seldom got a chance to put white supremacists in their place. His friend Bones hated rednecks; Willis hated skinheads.

The plan was a risky one, but Zoe was willing. Her sudden determination to return to the place where plant was grown and manufactured, coupled with her rage at the man who'd nabbed her, fueled her determination. "Don't worry," she said to Willis, pulling up her shirt to reveal her flat belly and tying it off. "They won't know what hit them."

"I'm counting on that." Willis brandished the length of pipe he'd found nearby.

As if suddenly transformed, Zoe's eyes glazed over, her smile widened, and she ambled through the door.

Willis peered through as Zoe meandered up to the surprised skinheads.

"Hey," she said. "Anybody got some…" She paused,

rubbed her face, wobbled a little. "Got some…"

The largest skinhead, a burly fellow with a red mustache, cackled. "Looks like we got us a crack whore wanting a fix. Come here girl, I'll fix you." He reached out, encircled her waist in his powerful arm, and pulled her onto his lap.

"Can you hook me up?" Zoe slurred.

"Course I can, if you're sweet to me." The man grinned at his friends. "Fellows, I think this whore is wearing entirely too many clothes. You want to help her out with that?"

Grinning lasciviously, the two men stood and closed in on Zoe.

That was when Willis sprang into action. He dashed forward, closing the gap in a split-second, and cracked the nearest skinhead across the chin with the pipe. The man dropped like a sack of potatoes. The second fared no better, catching the pipe across his temple.

And then something crashed into him, sending him stumbling backward and knocking the pipe from his hands. The biggest skinhead had lifted Zoe bodily and thrown her at Willis. That hadn't been part of the plan. Zoe had a knife, and was supposed to stab the man as soon as Willis appeared. Now he saw the knife in the skinhead's hand. The big man was advancing toward him, his bearing that of someone who knew how to fight.

Willis had disarmed plenty of men with knives in his time, but he was in a hurry, and pissed off to boot. He snatched the nearest bowling ball and flung it at the skinhead's leg. It cracked the man across the kneecap, eliciting a howl of pain. But Willis had already flung another, this one striking the shin. The skinhead went down on one knee and Willis snapped a roundhouse kick that caught him in the jaw.

The big man fell hard on his side. He struggled to rise, but his arms and legs weren't quite ready to cooperate. He looked up, eyes wild with rage and fear, as Willis loomed over him, holding a bowling ball high over his head.

"I bet this wasn't the first time you had big, black balls flying at your face."

As the skinhead slashed out with the knife, Willis brought the bowling ball down on the man's head with a sickening thud.

Not wasting time, he collected the bowling balls he'd used as weapons, wiped them down with a greasy rag he found nearby, and rolled them to the end of one of the lanes farther along. Next, he pressed the pistol into the hand of one of the skinheads, careful not to get blood or his fingerprints on it, then tossed it on the ground nearby.

Meanwhile, Zoe had freed the imprisoned young man, who stood rubbing his wrists and gazing at Willis in wonderment.

"Man, that was some World Star Hip Hop shit. I wish I had that on video." He saw the look in Willis' eyes and hurried on. "Just cause you kicked ass, you know? I ain't a snitch. You saved my life."

"And your nuts," Willis said. "You got a name?"

"Trey." The young man glowered at the fallen skinheads. "I owe them something." Picking up Zoe's knife, which was lying near the man with the red mustache, he dispatched the other two skinheads, opening their throats with a clinical detachment.

"There," he said, dropping the knife into a pool of blood, "now we're even. We gonna get out of here?"

Willis shook his head. "We got something to do."

The young man looked skeptical. "Y'all sure? There's

some crazy stuff going on around here. The ground shakes and I hear these moans coming out of the vents. Like ghosts or something."

"Ain't no ghosts," Willis said, "just assclowns."

"I don't know. This place has always been bad news. I heard the Indians wouldn't come nowhere near here. My grandma said they had a legend that this place stole their dreams, whatever that means. Anyhow, white folks came along and they didn't listen."

"There's a surprise," Zoe said.

Trey forced a crooked smile. "Well, thanks again. I'm out of here." He hurried away.

Willis watched him go, then turned to Zoe. "Lead the way."

The steam tunnel was not remotely steamy. Instead, it was surprisingly hot and dry as they made the monotonous trek to the underground lab. He stole the occasional glance at Zoe. Her expression was strained, and she occasionally pressed her hand to her forehead and muttered about a headache.

From up ahead came the strange sounds Trey had described. Deep, anguished moans. As they drew closer, Willis felt a chill. He knew tunnels like this could cause strange reverberations, lending an unearthly touch to commonplace sounds. But these sounds were hardly common.

"Sounds like somebody's in pain up there. A bunch of somebodies. What do they do in this lab? Are they testing the drug on people?"

"I don't remember," Zoe said, much too fast.

Willis eyed her with rising apprehension. Something was very wrong about this whole situation, something that went beyond dealers putting a strange, new drug on the street. Furthermore, he didn't believe Zoe was sick. At least, not with any commonplace illness. Perhaps she'd tried this new drug, plant, and was suffering the side-effects? A flickering light cast a sickly yellow glow, giving Zoe a jaundiced look. As they passed beneath it, he noticed a lump at the center of her forehead. Had it been there before?

"Did that skinhead punch you?" He reached out to touch her head and she swatted his hand away.

"Don't touch me." She took a step back. "We're almost there. It's up around the corner."

The way she said "it" told him she wasn't referring to the lab.

Just then, a shrill scream split the air. The sound of a woman terrified out of her wits. "No! Please!"

Willis hurried ahead but Zoe grabbed him around the waist like a football player trying to make a tackle. "Girl, what are you doing? Somebody's in trouble up there."

"She's already dead." Tears streamed down Zoe's face. "It's all wrong in there. I saw stuff nobody should ever see."

"You wanted to come back."

"I think I have to." She began to tremble. "I ate some of the plant." Her voice was a sharp hiss.

"Ate it? Why?"

"I wanted to try it, but I couldn't take any of the powder. They're real particular about it. Weigh it when they give it to you and then again when you deliver it." She hesitated. "There's these parts that grow at the tips of the plant, like red fingers. That's the part they turn into powder. There was a bunch of it they'd just harvested. It was lying there and I just broke off a little bit of it."

Willis couldn't believe she had been so stupid. "You

said you just did this for the money."

"I was stupid, I know. But I saw…" She looked down, unable to meet his eye.

"What?"

"I saw into Lonzo's memories. For real."

Willis rolled his eyes. "The drug made you think that."

Zoe gave her head a vigorous shake, her tight, black curls falling across her eyes. "I saw you both. You were just out of school. You robbed an old man right out on the street, and then you punched him. Knocked him out cold."

Willis swayed on the spot. It was one of his most shameful memories—the incident that convinced him to change his life by joining the Navy.

"Lonzo told you about that," he said hoarsely.

"I saw it."

"I don't have time for this. Just stay here." He turned and strode along the tunnel, toward the place from which the screams had come seconds before. A red glow filled the passageway, and the heat grew intense. He turned the corner and stopped short.

He stood before a heavy door with a small security window. Inside lay a vision from a nightmare.

The plant was a monstrosity, alien in appearance. It stood at least twenty feet tall and forty or more feet across. A plexiglass dome hung suspended from the ceiling, sheltering it from the groundwater that dripped down from countless cracks. The plant's dark green stem was so thick that Willis could not have wrapped his arms around it. It flowered at the top in a series of shovel-shaped petals so black they seemed to swallow the red light. Black spikes studded its length. But that wasn't the most disturbing part. Growing out from the stem were long vines covered in gray, worm-like tendrils, some ending in the red tips that Zoe had described, others with mouths like a Venus flytrap. And they were moving.

Another scream rang out, harsh and strident, and Willis saw a burly man shove a young woman toward the twisting vines. She tried to run, but one of the mouths clamped down on her head and pulled her into the mass of writhing green. She cried out as two of the red spikes wormed into her ears. Eyes still on the woman, Willis tried the door and found it locked.

He stepped back and threw his shoulder into the door once, twice, three times. The door was solid but Willis was a powerfully built man, and he kept in shape through a rigorous exercise regimen and lots of SCUBA diving. The fourth try and the door gave way. He stumbled inside, his eyes taking it all in.

The floor was a white latticework of what he quickly recognized as layer upon layer of bones—human and animals of all kind. How long had this plant been down here, feeding? He circled the massive thing, careful not to come within reach of its tentacles. Now he saw the bodies. Some were in an advanced state of decay, others still alive, though in what appeared to be a comatose state. Each victim was held in place by one of the horrible jaw-like appendages which appeared to have melded with the flesh, making the person a part of the plant. Other vines grew from their ears.

"It's feeding on them," he muttered. The pieces began to fall into place. This plant absorbed its victims, consumed them. That was why it didn't need water.

And then he spotted Lonzo. His cousin lay within the grasp of the plant. His eyes were milky white, his mouth hung open. Like the other victims, the plant had melded with his skull, and vines had penetrated his ears. And then he remembered his conversation with Zoe earlier.

"Is Lonzo carrying, like you, or is he involved in the growing?"

"He's growing."

He hadn't realized how literal Zoe's words were. And then he thought about the effect of the drug. Was it possible that the plant somehow absorbed its victims' memories? After all, what were memories but electrical currents and chemical reactions? Maybe Zoe really had gotten a brief window into Lonzo's memories.

And then he remembered something else she had said.

"I'm sure Lonzo is long gone by now."

"Aw man, Lonzo," Willis groaned. "Ain't a damn thing I can do for you." Nor could he help anyone else. The young woman he'd seen being fed to the plant was already catatonic, though still letting out intermittent shrieks and cries.

"This is where the urban legend came from. Must have been a cavern down here where this thing lived, and people heard its victims crying out."

Something moved at the corner of his vision. Zoe had followed him! In his utter shock at seeing the horrifying spectacle, he'd forgotten his friend. Now she moved, trancelike, toward the flailing vines. The plant seemed to register her presence. Three of the appendages turned in her direction and reached out for her.

"Zoe! What the hell are you doing?" He dashed toward her, seized her by the arm, and yanked her back just as a pair of green jaws snapped shut, inches from her face.

"Let me go. I have to go to it."

"You crazy?"

"Yes! And I'm not going to get better." She began to shake. "Look at my head. It's inside me."

The lump on her forehead had grown, and was moving, as if something inside struggled to get out. And then a red spike burst forth in a spray of blood. Instinctively Willis jumped back, and in doing so, released his grip on her arm.

Zoe didn't hesitate. She turned and ran into the arms of the horrifying thing that waited to consume her.

"Zoe!"

Nausea swept over him as he watched the plant embrace her in its sinister coils. He took a step toward her, and then danced back from its searching grasp. He knew she was gone and so was Lonzo, but he had to do something about this monstrosity.

He made his way to the door leading to the lab. Inside, a burly man, pistol on his hip, stood with his back to Willis. Beyond him, two men wearing goggles, masks, and gloves were hard at work. All around them were the trappings of a drug lab. He recognized various acids and chemicals. Based on what he saw, he had a feeling they were also cooking meth here, or had done so in the recent past.

Heart racing, he tried the door. It was unlocked. Slowly, silently, he turned the handle and opened the door. He was just about to squeeze through when the hinges let out a loud squeak.

The armed man turned toward him, but much too slowly. Willis drove a sharp punch into the man's Adam 's apple, then followed with a left hook to the jaw that turned his legs to water. The masked men froze, eyes wide behind their goggles. One of them raised his hands above his head and the other followed suit.

"If you're a cop, we'll cooperate," one said. "And if you're not, just take what you want. We won't try to stop you."

"I ain't no cop." Willis knelt and freed the fallen man's pistol from its holster. He confirmed the safety was off and a round was in the chamber. "And the only thing I want is for this mess to end." Horrible images flashed through his mind, visions of Lonzo, Zoe, and all the other victims being consumed by the plant. Rage burning inside him he raised the pistol and aimed it at the chest of the nearest man. "What the hell is that thing?

"Can't say for sure. Lance thinks it's alien. Said there was a legend of a meteor landing in the marsh hundreds of years ago. A local Indian tribe took it down into this cavern, treated it like it was sacred. That didn't work out so well for them."

"How do I kill it?"

The man shrugged. "We're chemists, not botanists." He glanced down at a graduated cylinder filled with red powder. "Look, dude, there's plenty of this to go around. This right here is worth thousands. Just take it and we'll forget we ever met one another." He picked up the glass container and, with a sudden flick of the wrist, flung it in Willis' direction.

Willis had expected the man to pull something. He dodged a few steps to the side and squeezed off two shots, taking one chemist in the heart and the other in the forehead. The guard whom Willis had knocked out earlier began to cough as the cloud of fine powder settled around him. Willis decided not to waste a bullet on him just yet. He had to deal with the plant, and he had an idea how.

Moving out of the lab, he looked up at the plexiglass

dome. Zoe had said it was essential that the drug not get wet, and clearly the plant itself was being shielded from the water. He took aim and fired. The impact smashed a jagged hole in the dome and water began to drizzle down onto the plant. Where it struck, the plant began to violently flail about.

"You don't like that, do you?"

He continued to fire at the dome until he'd emptied the magazine. Water dripped down from half a dozen gaping holes in the protective cover. The entire plant writhed, and its human victims, those who still had a voice, let out high-pitched screams. But was it enough? The plant seemed to be angry, but still very much alive. Maybe immersion in water would do the trick, but that wasn't an option. There had to be another way.

The lab! He ran back inside and began gathering up the ingredients he would need. He made several trips, proceeding cautiously as he cooked up the deadly cocktail: hypophosphorous acid, lithium metal, acetone, anything he could find. Some he mixed, others he sat side by side in strategic locations all around the cavern. Then came the flammables until he had created a trail leading to the exit door. Casting one last, regretful look at Zoe and Lonzo, he lit the fire and ran.

Behind him he heard a whoosh and a roar. Golden light filled the tunnel, and then a deafening explosion hurled him off his feet. He hit the ground face-first, smashing his nose and forcing the air from his lungs. Chunks of concrete fell all around him. The tunnel was coming down. He had to get out of there.

Forcing himself to his feet, he half-ran, half-reeled to the pile of rubble that provided egress into the bowling alley. He began to climb. Another tremor shook the passageway, shifting the loose debris beneath his feet. He slid back to the floor, a falling chunk of ceiling just missing him.

"Where's my crew when I need them?" he rasped. He began to climb again, rocks shifting beneath his feet, dust choking his lungs. He climbed up, slid down, and climbed again. His strength waned. The way out seemed to remain just out of his reach.

"Almost there!" he gasped. He reached for the opening, but another tremor sent him sliding back.

And then someone caught his outstretched hand in a firm grip. "I can't pull you out," a familiar voice said. "You got to help me."

Unable to believe his luck, Willis threw the last of his energy into the effort. Grunting from the effort, he climbed free of the collapsing tunnel, and found himself face to face with Trey.

"Now we're even," Trey said.

"Thanks. Now we gotta get out of here," Willis replied, and they began to run.

Ground trembling beneath their feet, they dashed out of the bowling alley and into the dank night air. They didn't stop running until they reached his car.

"What the hell happened down there?" Trey asked.

Willis grimaced. "One big ass meth lab explosion."

"A meth lab? You mean there wasn't anything else? No aliens? No ghosts?"

"No, man," Willis said. "That was all just an urban legend."

The End

AZTLAN

Maddock and Bones go rock climbing in a remote area of the American Southwest and stumble upon a place out of legend that changes their world.

"Aztlan" is a short story that takes place after the events of *Atlantis*. I wrote it as a bonus for the first *Dane Maddock Adventures* boxed set and I later included it in the first Bones novella, *Primitive*.

"Holy crap, it's hot out here." Bones Bonebrake mopped his brow and cast a challenging look at the sun high in the cornflower blue sky. "And don't give me that 'It's a dry heat' stuff. Hot is hot."

"No argument here." Dane Maddock plucked at the neck of his sodden shirt. It wouldn't stay damp for long in this dry climate. He hunkered down on the tiny rock ledge where they'd stopped to take a breather, took a bottle of water from his pack, and took a long drink. He gazed out at the parched red landscape of southern Utah. Sharp peaks and low hills dotted the horizon, all shades of the same reddish-brown as the mountainside on which they perched. It had been a long time since he'd ventured into this part of the country, and he realized he'd missed the open skies and sweeping vistas.

"Are we close to the top?"

"Why? Are you ready to wuss out on me?" Bones' heavy breathing belied his bravado.

"Hardly. We both know I'll reach the summit before you do. Why don't you just give it up?"

"Not on your life." The tall, powerfully-built Cherokee squatted down beside Maddock, removed the tie from around his ponytail, and let his long hair blow in the breeze.

The two made an odd pair: Maddock was fair-skinned with blue eyes and short, blond hair. He stood just a shade under six feet tall, but alongside the six and a half foot tall Bones, he looked small.

Bones stood, knuckled his back, and turned to examine the rock face above them. "Only about fifty meters to go. Shouldn't be too bad."

"Remind me again why we decided to free climb here?" Maddock asked, tucking the water bottle back into his pack and rising to his feet.

"Because no one ever has. Because it's awesome." Bones bared his straight white teeth in a wolfish grin.

"How'd you find out about this place, anyway?"

"My cousin Isaiah." Bones' cousin, Isaiah Horsely, was a professor and archaeologist working the American Southwest. "He found out about it from a local storyteller who says few people even know this place exists."

"I don't wonder," Maddock said. "Considering how much trouble we had just getting here, much less climbing it."

Motec Mountain's height and steep sides made it look less like a mountain and more like a butte that had been stretched out until it touched the sky. Nestled in the heart of Utah's Red Rock region, it was one of the most remote locations Maddock had ever visited in this part of the country.

"He told me some other stuff about it. Legends mostly. Weird stuff but pretty cool."

"Tell me when we get to the top. The longer I stand here, the more I think about the cooler of beer waiting in the car."

"Dude, you can drink beer any time. How often do you get to boldly go where not very many men have gone before?"

Maddock frowned at Bones. "Seriously? We do it all the time."

"And that's why we rule. Now let's get back to climbing."

Upon reaching the summit, Maddock expected to be rewarded with a refreshing breeze and a spectacular view, but he found neither. A fine mist hung over the landscape, slowly swirling in a clockwise pattern and giving the air a tepid quality.

"This is weird." Bones waved his hand in front of his face, the mist curling around his arm. "It's like it wants to grab ahold of you."

"Nothing about this makes sense," Maddock said. "We're in an arid climate. Why doesn't the fog dissipate, or at least burn off? And where is the moisture coming from?"

"The storyteller said there's a lake up here. Want to check it out?"

Maddock gazed at the curtain of mist. It was odd, to be sure, but it didn't seem to be dangerous. Curiosity winning out over caution, he nodded. "Let's see what's up."

The way was smooth, with only a few scattered boulders here and there to impede their way. Though the mist shrouded the landscape in white, it was thin and visibility was more than adequate. Soon they came to the edge of a dark lake.

"Want to go for a swim?" Bones asked.

"I don't know." Maddock felt uneasy as he scanned the surface of the water. He realized in an instant what caused his discomfort. "The water doesn't move at all. Look at it. It's like a sheet of glass."

"Maybe it is." Bones knelt down and touched the surface. It scarcely made a ripple. "This is jacked-up. It's water, all right, but it's like there's a surface tension holding it in place. I don't know how to describe it."

"I think you describe it just fine," Maddock said,

dipping his own finger into the water. "It's warm, too."

"Isn't there a lake in the Middle East where people float really easily?" Bones asked. "You know, like without an inner tube or those water wings you love?"

"The Dead Sea." Maddock ignored his friend's jibe. "But that's because of the high salt content. I don't think that's the deal here."

"If it's all the same to you, I'm not going to taste the water." Bones wiped his hand on his shirt.

"And I think we'll pass on the swimming, too."

They stood and began to walk along the shore. They quickly discovered the lake was perfectly round, or something close to perfect. As they walked, Maddock's discomfort lessened. Maybe this place was more odd than sinister. Nonetheless, he took a moment to dig into his pack for the dive knife he always carried, and hooked the sheath onto his belt. Bones did the same, and they continued their exploration of the mountaintop.

Maddock estimated they'd reached the side of the lake opposite where they'd begun their circuit when Bones halted in his tracks.

"Look at this."

Maddock followed his friend's line of sight to where a complete skeleton grinned up at them. A tarnished breastplate covered its chest and a tarnished helmet and the rusted remains of a sword lay nearby.

"Spanish," Maddock noted. "Probably an explorer."

"And he climbed all the way up here in his armor?" Bones said doubtfully. "I'm not buying it."

"It wouldn't be the strangest thing we've seen. Who knows? Maybe there is, or was, another way up."

"I have another idea." Bones folded his arms and turned to face Maddock. "Hear me out on this. This is an alien hot zone." He raised a big hand before Maddock could argue. "Just listen. That could explain the weird water and the mist. And like you said, we've seen enough strange crap that it's not the most far-fetched idea in the world."

"So the aliens abducted the Spaniard and then dumped him here?" Maddock couldn't believe he was indulging his friend's fixation with extraterrestrials, but Bones wasn't wrong. They'd seen and experienced enough strange things that nothing could be discounted.

"Now you're thinking like an honest-to-goodness conspiracy theorist. I knew I'd win you over sooner or later."

"Just trying to follow your train of thought, and believe me, it's a scary ride."

They continued on and made it only twenty or so paces before something on the lake caught Maddock's attention.

"Bones, look at that." Far from the shore, a dark shape loomed in the mist. At their feet, flat round stepping stones formed a bridge.

"Another of the storyteller's details I forgot to mention," Bones said. "There's supposed to be an island in the middle of the lake. And, of course, it's cursed."

"Do you believe in curses?" Maddock asked.

"Other than a woman scorned? Nope." Bones grinned. "Lead the way."

Maddock tested the first stepping stone and found it was solid. He tensed slightly as he put his full weight on it, and relaxed when it held. "I don't know if it'll support your fat butt," he said to Bones, "but I'm good to go."

"Screw you, Maddock."

Maddock almost felt like he was dreaming as he

moved through the mist across the motionless lake.

"I bet this is what Heaven is like," Bones said in an uncharacteristically soft voice.

"You'll never find out."

"That's cool. Better parties in hell, anyway."

At the center of the lake, they stepped onto solid stone. It didn't take long to discover that what Bones had believed to be an island was, in fact, a giant stone disc.

"I told you, dude," Bones said. "Aliens."

"Aztecs, more like. See?"

Symbols and other imagery covered the rock beneath their feet. Though he didn't know the meanings of most of them, the patterns and motifs were familiar. "It looks like a giant Aztec Calendar Stone."

"You're right." Bones dropped to one knee to get a closer look. "Doesn't mean aliens didn't help them, though."

"True. Let's keep going."

They moved deeper into the mist and soon the dark form toward which they'd been moving began to take shape. They soon found themselves at the foot of a miniature pyramid. At the top stood a small temple, surmounted by a sculpture of the feathered serpent head of Quetzalcoatl. That sealed it. The site was definitely Aztec.

They climbed the dozen stairs to the top, where, just inside the temple door, a tight spiral staircase descended into the darkness. They clicked on their mini Maglites and headed down. Time seemed to slow as they wound deeper into the heart of the mountain, Bones grumbling all the while about the low ceiling and tight quarters.

Finally, they emerged into a large chamber. Maddock halted at the entrance and ran the beam of his light across the floor, looking for potential booby traps, but saw nothing. He took a few cautious steps inside and waited for Bones to join him.

"Interesting," Bones observed, shining his light all around.

The room was round with a low ceiling. Spaced equally were the mouths of seven caves. At the center stood a waist-high pedestal.

"There's an Aztec legend," Bones began, "about a place called Chicomoztoc, or 'The Place of the Seven Caves.' From here, seven tribes, for lack of a better term, came together and settled at Aztlan, the ancestral home of the Aztecs."

"So if this is Chicomoztoc, then you think Aztlan is somewhere around here?" Maddock asked.

"The Aztecs called Aztlan 'The land to the North', and this is well north of Mexico. It was reputed to be an island within a lake." Bones scratched his chin. "And the word itself means 'the place of whiteness.' Think about it: the island within a lake, the white mist, the connection to the caves. I think the island up above us is Aztlan."

Maddock frowned. "But Aztlan is supposed to be the Aztecs' ancestral home. An entire nation couldn't live up there. It's just a single mountaintop."

"You know how legends work. They get passed down from generation-to-generation and it changes a little at a time until it's an entirely different story with only a few recognizable details remaining. Maybe Aztlan was the place the Aztecs emerged from, I don't know, under the earth."

Only a few years earlier Maddock would have scoffed at this, but such a story no longer seemed far-fetched. "Let's check out the caves."

They began by exploring the first cave to their left and quickly discovered that it plunged downward at a steep angle, going on and on with no end in sight. A cursory inspection of the other caves produced similar results.

"This isn't a two-man job," Maddock concluded. "It would take a team, maybe several teams, of researchers to explore this place, depending on how far down the caves go." He turned and shined his light on the pedestal at the center of the main chamber. "Let's check this out."

At first glance, the pedestal was merely a simple cylinder, but closer inspection revealed a detail that had gone unnoticed. At the top, set in the center of the cylinder, was a turquoise disc.

No more than a hand's length across, it was engraved with several symbols. Around the outside ran what looked like a seven-lobed clover. Inside that lay a ring of five suns. Finally, at the center, two figures faced one another. Only a few minor details kept them from being mirror images of one another. The images meant nothing to Maddock, but Bones gasped when his light fell on them.

"Holy crap, Maddock. I know what this is!"

Maddock was not surprised that Bones had some knowledge of Aztec lore. His friend had a keen interest in myths, legends, and ancient prophecies, and the Aztecs were strongly associated with the end of days, and also with aliens, another of Bones' favorite subjects.

"This," he said, hovering a finger over the cloverlike outline, "represents the seven caves. The sunbursts symbolize the five suns of creation. And they," he pointed at the figures in the center, "are Ometecuhtli and his female partner, Omecíhuatl, the highest of the Aztec deities." He looked at Maddock. "This is the Duality Stone."

"What the hell does that mean?"

"I can't say for sure. Only the craziest conspiracy theorist believes it exists." He broke out into a broad grin. "Tell me again what nutbags those guys are."

"You know what they say about a blind squirrel," Maddock said. "But in this case, I tip my cap to you and your eccentric friends."

Bones stood for several moments in silent contemplation. "I think we should tell Isaiah about this place. After all, he's the one who tipped me off about it, and he's got the resources to study it properly.

"Agreed," Maddock said. "This is one heck of a discovery."

The sun was setting over the hills, painting the landscape in shades of orange, by the time they made it back to their vehicle. Both men were utterly spent, yet buoyed by their discovery, their spirits remained high. As they drove along the rutted dirt road back to civilization, Bones spied a small bar. It was a squat, adobe style building of faded brown, nearly the color of the surrounding earth. A faded sign, the paint peeling, proclaimed it the White Bear Pub.

"I don't remember seeing that place on the way here," Bones said. "It's not often a watering hole escapes my notice."

"It was six in the morning. I hope you weren't keeping an eye out for bars," Maddock said.

Bones nodded thoughtfully. "That must be it. Let's stop for a while."

"We've got beer in the cooler."

"Yeah, but this place has different beer. No reason we can't drink both."

Bones slowed and turned off the main road. He parked alongside the only other vehicle in the dirt lot— an aging sedan of unfamiliar make. As they mounted the single, rickety step up to the building, he glanced back at their rented SUV and frowned.

"I could have sworn we rented a CRV," he said.

"I thought so too." Maddock walked around the back of the vehicle to check the model name. "What the hell is a GAZelle?"

Bones shrugged. "Who knows? Must be a Hyundai or some crap like that. It got us here. That's what matters."

Inside, they found themselves the lone customers inside the dusty bar. Narrow beams of sunlight filtered in through dirty windows, shining on the ceramic tile floor, which was pitted and cracked in places, and setting the dust motes aglow. Maddock and Bones took seats at the bar where the local news was showing on an aging television set.

"Couldn't spring for a flat screen?" Bones asked.

"Don't worry about it."

The bartender, a stout man of late middle years with lightly tanned skin, copious ear hair, and a bald head, greeted them enthusiastically.

"My first customers of the day. I am Alexei. What can I get you?"

Maddock noted a slight Russian accent to the man's speech. Unusual for this part of the country.

"Dos cervezas, por favor." Bones held up two fingers. "Dos Equis if you've got it."

Alexei frowned. "I don't know this beer."

"That's cool. Just give us two of the best beers you've

got."

The man smiled and handed them two bottles labeled Tinkoff Golden. Bones tipped him generously and clinked bottles with Maddock. "To discovery."

"Discovery," Maddock agreed. He took a long drink, taking the time to savor the light, tangy flavor. He nodded approvingly and took another drink. "Not bad."

They finished their drinks quickly and Bones called out to the bartender. "Yo, Axel. Another round."

"Alexei," the man corrected though he smiled to show no offense was taken.

"Who's your pick to win the Superbowl this year?" Bones asked, trying to make conversation.

Alexei tilted his head. "You mean the Soccerbowl?"

"What? No, dude. The Superbowl. Football."

"Football and soccer are the same." Alexei picked up a greasy rag and began wiping the counter. "Or do you mean gridiron?" Bones nodded and Alexei grimaced. "Nasty, violent sport. I didn't think they played it anymore."

Bones made a confused face but continued to make small talk with Alexei. Meanwhile, Maddock turned his attention to the television, where the reporter was saying, "Today the American Politburo sent a strongly-worded message to Moscow, warning the Premier that America will not be treated as a lesser member of the Soviet Union."

Maddock almost spilled his beer. Bones had heard too.

"Are we on a hidden camera show?" Bones looked around.

"I don't understand your jokes," Alexei said, "but I like you all the same."

"You're pretty cool too," Bones said. "Say, who's the president nowadays?"

Alexei cocked his head. "How do you not know that?"

"I can't really talk about it. Let's just say I've been out of circulation for a while."

"No television in prison?" Alexei grinned. "The president is Vladimir Putin."

"I meant the President of the United States."

Alexei laughed. "Now I think I am the one on hidden camera. There has been no president since the war. The American Politburo governs but reports to Moscow, just like all countries in the Soviet Union."

Maddock's head swam and he felt as though his tether to reality was slipping. He took a closer look at their surroundings, truly taking in all the details. Everything was Russian—posters of soccer and hockey teams and framed photographs of Soviet premiers dominated the walls.

Alexei walked away, shaking his head, and Maddock looked at Bones.

"What the hell is going on here?"

Bones stared at him, and then he closed his eyes and let out a groan. "I did it." He buried his face in his hands. "I took the duality stone. It's in my pack. I don't know why I did it. It was like the stone wanted to be taken."

Maddock was surprised at what Bones had done, but that wasn't his primary concern at the moment. "Why should that matter?" he asked.

Bones sighed. "According to legend, the duality stone holds the worlds together." He shook his head. "No, that's not quite right. More like, it tethers the different versions of the world."

"Different versions?"

"You know, like alternate timelines. I know it sounds nuts, but I think it's taken us to a timeline where the Russians won the Cold War."

Maddock looked at the label on his beer and considered what Bones said. Unless they were both experiencing the same hallucination, nothing else made sense. "Maybe we're dreaming," he said lamely.

A sharp pain blossomed in his shoulder. Bones had punched him. "What the hell?"

"Does that feel like a dream?" Bones asked.

"I don't know. Does this?" He returned the favor and Bones winced.

"Okay. We can rule out dreaming."

Alexei, who was polishing the end of the counter, scowled at them. "You fight outside. Not here."

Maddock was about to apologize when his phone vibrated. He looked at it and his jaw dropped.

"You all right, bro? You're pale as a… well, as a you."

"I just got a text. From Melissa."

Bones looked poleaxed. "That can't be right."

Melissa was Maddock's wife who had died years before.

"If we're in an alternate timeline, maybe she's…" Maddock couldn't say it aloud. Holding his phone in a trembling hand, he read the message aloud.

Hope you can come home soon. We miss you.

"We," he whispered. "Melissa was pregnant when she died. Maybe…"

"Don't do this to yourself, Maddock," Bones said.

Maddock scarcely heard him. He was scrolling through his contact list. He saw familiar names: Bones,

Matt Barnaby, Willis Sanders, Pete "Professor" Chapman, Corey Dean, and Jimmy Letson.

But he also saw names that hadn't been there before: Hartford Maxwell, their old commander who had been murdered by the Dominion. Franklin Meriwether, a beloved officer who had died in the Holy Land, and then he gasped.

"Mom and Dad," he breathed. "Bones, look at this! My parents are still alive, and Maxie and Meriwether."

Bones snatched the phone away and scrolled through the list, his brow furrowing deeper as he read. "This is not good."

"What do you mean? Melissa, my parents! Bones, I need to go home."

"Just chill for a second. Listen, we don't belong here. Right now, some alternate Maddock is probably driving home from his job selling insurance, and I'm sure there's another version of Bones who's getting busy with a Russian tennis player. But they're not us and we aren't them."

"How do you know? Maybe the alternate version of us are on a climbing trip in Utah. Maybe we've taken their places."

"It doesn't matter. This isn't our world. Look at this." Bones turned Maddock's phone around so he could see the display. "Yeah, there are some new names here, but you know what? There are some missing too. Matt and Corey aren't here. That means we don't have a crew. There's no Kaylin Maxwell, no Jade, no Tam Broderick. All those mysteries we solved? All we did to fight the Dominion? Never happened. Not here. And there's another important name missing."

They exchanged a level look and Maddock felt his

resistance crumbling. He knew precisely who Bones meant. Pain stabbed at his heart. He knew he couldn't stay here but how could he leave?

"Besides, do you really want to live here, under Soviet rule?"

Maddock shook his head. "I suppose not."

Just then, the phone vibrated again. Bones glanced at it and his eyes went wide.

"What is it?"

Bones shook his head. "You're better off not knowing. Trust me."

"Give it to me." Maddock spoke slowly, pronouncing each syllable in a tone that said he would brook no nonsense. Reluctantly, Bones handed it over.

Melissa had texted him again. This time she'd sent a photograph. There she was, her smile and her big brown eyes were just as he remembered. But it was the little boy, a blue-eyed blond who sat on her knee, that captivated him. It was his son.

"He looks just like you," Bones said.

Maddock's throat was tight and he only managed a single nod. He felt as if his heart were being torn into a million pieces. It was more than he could take. He took a deep breath and cleared his throat. When he could finally speak, his voice was husky.

"Bones, let's put that stone back where we found it."

The moon hung low on the horizon when they once again emerged from the temple atop Motec Mountain. It shone dully through the mist that still hung over the mountaintop. Between the climbing and the strain of this afternoon's experience, Maddock had nothing left. He crossed the lake and made his way back to the spot where they'd made their ascent only scarcely aware of his surroundings, his mind as foggy as the air that surrounded them.

"I think we should stay here until morning," Bones said. "It's too dark and we're both too tired to climb down."

Maddock nodded and sank to the ground.

"It sucks that we won't know until tomorrow whether we made it home or if we're still stuck in our own version of Red Dawn."

Maddock took out his phone. He scrolled through the contact list and then checked the text messages. The photo and message from Melissa were gone. His list was back to normal, though, and the name at the top brought a smile to his face— Angel.

His phone vibrated. Angel had sent him a text message.

Are you assclowns staying out of trouble?

Maddock laughed "It's all right," he said. "We're back."

THE END

PHANTOM ISLAND

When the island of Bermeja suddenly vanished from world maps, government officials said it was a "Phantom Island"—one which had erroneously appeared on historical maps, but was later found not to exist. A hunting expedition takes Matt Barnaby to the legendary Phantom Island, and into the path of its deadly denizens.

This short story originally appeared in a different form under the title "Lost Island" in the Severed Press anthology *Prehistoric.*

PHANTOM ISLAND

"Is it me, or does the way ahead look a little strange?" Matt Barnaby looked out at the fog blanketing the cobalt waters of the Gulf of Mexico. It was late morning, the sun bright and the temperature warm, yet the fog remained.

"Lighten up. Just because you spend all your time lounging on your boss's boat doesn't make you a weatherman," his brother, Kevin, chided. Kevin never missed a chance to needle him. Kevin had gone into the family business, while Matt had chosen the Army, followed by a life of treasure hunting. Both had kept him far from Minnesota and his family.

"It's just weird, that's all." Matt turned his back on the curtain of gray into which they were headed. "The fog should have burned off by now."

"The place we're headed is unusual. The weather is the least of it." If his father, Robert "Doc" Barnaby, found the phenomenon unnerving, he didn't let it show.

"It will be fine," Kevin said. "You're going to love this, bro. It will take your mind off of… what is your job, again?"

"Marine archaeologist."

Kevin shrugged, turned, and opened the cooler. "Who wants a cold one?" Without waiting for an answer, he handed a bottle to his father and tossed another to Matt.

"This is nice," Doc said. "A father-son trip with both of my boys. How long has it been?"

"Before I enlisted. But it's not like you never see me," Matt hurriedly added. Despite the distance he had intentionally created between them, Matt still visited regularly and enjoyed his time with his mother and sisters. He could even tolerate Doc and Kevin in small doses. He simply had no desire to travel with them.

"That's right." Doc scratched his chin. "Spring break of your junior year. We were climbing El Capitan. That was when you finally told me what your actual career plan was."

"Give him a break, Pops," Kevin said. "If he wants to spend his life trying to be Dirk Pitt, that's his business."

Matt didn't rise. It was territory they'd covered countless times before. Neither of his chosen careers had been lucrative, but they'd been the right choice for him. And he had no interest in being Executive Vice President in Charge of Bullshit at Barnaby Foods, especially considering what their real business was.

Doc and Kevin exchanged a long, knowing look. If Kevin had been thirty years older, the pair might have been twins—blonde, blue eyed, sturdily built. Matt was the black sheep, or "brown sheep" as his brother called him. Of the five Barnaby children, only Matt had chestnut hair and brown eyes. He also stood a few inches taller and weighed in about twenty pounds heavier than his father or brother.

Kevin turned to Doc. "By the way, Pops, did you ever get his name?"

Doc frowned. "Whose name?"

"The milkman who knocked up Mom."

The two laughed out loud and clinked beer bottles. Matt force a grin. It was only the ten thousandth time they'd made that same joke.

A chill passed over him, and he realized they had moved into the fog bank. The cool dampness clung to his skin, and cast his father and brother in a haze like looking through filmy gauze.

"Almost there!" Doc raised his beer and clinked bottles with his sons. "To a successful hunt."

"Cheers." Kevin grinned.

"Cheers," Matt echoed dully. He hadn't hunted in years, but his father had practically begged him to come along on this expedition, promising it would be the trip of a lifetime.

"Okay, Pops. Don't you think it's about time you spilled the secret details? You haven't told me anything other than we're going on a hunt."

"What would you like to know?" Doc's grin crinkled the corners of his mouth.

"For starters, where are we going? What place is so secret that I had to sign a non-disclosure agreement before I could hunt there?"

"The island of Bermeja."

That brought Matt up short. "Bermeja? The Phantom Island?:

"Yes," Doc said.

"Bermeja isn't real! It showed up erroneously on some old charts. Mexico pretended it was real in order to stake claim to waters where oil was in good supply."

"Is that so?" Doc inclined his head, his brow furrowed. "You'll have to explain that to the men who live there."

"Is this a joke?" Matt asked. It would be just like his father and brother to wind him up with an absurd story.

"Would you listen to this guy?" Kevin said. "He and his buddies claim to have discovered Atlantis but he's skeptical about Bermeja?"

"I don't know what you're talking about." Matt maintained his poker face.

Kevin gave him a playful punch in the shoulder. "That's not what you told Selina. And that's not all. Hidden temples, lost treasure, ancient artifacts... Don't get me wrong, I've got no problem with lying to a girl to get her in the sack, but you shouldn't get all your stories from Indiana Jones."

Matt breathed a sigh of relief. It had been foolish of him to repeat those stories to his ex-girlfriend, but drinks and nostalgia had loosened his tongue. It was best for all concerned if everyone thought he'd been telling tall tales. He decided to change the subject and turned to his father.

"So, Bermeja is not just a myth?"

"Not at all. The legend of the 'lost' island is not factual, nor is the conspiracy theory that the CIA blew it up in order to thwart Mexico's claim on the surrounding waters. I assure you, it is quite real."

"But how?"

Doc flashed a knowing smile. "Money and power can do many things, even make an island disappear."

"Money," Kevin parroted, nodding along.

"The perpetual fog and the fact that the island is very small also helps," Doc added.

Matt wasn't satisfied. "But there have been independent surveys that confirmed it didn't exist."

Doc flashed Matt a pitying smile, then turned to Kevin. "Independent, he says." He turned his gaze back to Matt. "Son, you pay the right people, do a few favors, call in some markers, and there's not much that can't be accomplished. Mexico has a vested interest in keeping this island a secret. You'll soon find out why."

"Dinosaurs." Matt gazed at the horned skull that hung above the fireplace in the common room of the Bermeja Lodge. He wasn't certain of the species, Stegosaurus, maybe, but it was definitely a dinosaur, and not a fossil. This was bleached bone. Had it been a steer it wouldn't have been out of place in a ranch house in the American Southwest. "You're telling me we're going to hunt actual, walking, eating, breathing, living dinosaurs?"

"You will all have to excuse my brother. He's always slow on the uptake," Kevin announced to the room.

Laughter rang out from the group that sat in a semicircle on comfortable chairs, enjoying drinks.

"Is this an elaborate prank?" Matt looked around for hidden cameras or a B-list celebrity waiting to pop out and surprise them. He believed that some dinosaurs could still exist in very remote locations. Hell, his friend Bones Bonebrake had shown him evidence of one. What he couldn't wrap his head around was the idea that this island was large enough to support a population sufficient for trophy hunting.

"If so, we've all wasted a great deal of money for nothing." Albert Montez, a bear of a man with light brown skin and steel-gray hair cropped in a G.I. cut, was a Texas land baron or something like that. Beside him, his daughter Maya sat, sipping a glass of red wine, her expression unreadable.

Matt had gone out of his way not to stare at the young woman. It hadn't been easy. Even if she hadn't been the only female within hundreds of miles, her big brown eyes and trim, athletic figure would have drawn his attention in any setting. He had trouble reconciling a beautiful young woman with a trophy hunting expedition. He supposed that was gender stereotyping. Still, the thought made him a little sad.

Seated on the other side of Maya was Eric Barnard, a skinny, early twenties type with "trust fund kid" written all over him. His popped collar and loud proclamations about the superiority of craft beer over brand name brews had already alienated him from the rest of the group, but he appeared oblivious to their disdain.

Their team was rounded out by Harrison Tomlin, a tall, ebony skinned man, gray around the temples, with a wicked scar bisecting his left cheek. He would be their hunting guide. He drank little and said even less.

"You'll have to excuse my son," Doc said. "He fancies himself a scientist. I guess he doesn't believe in anything without testable evidence."

Matt didn't miss the subtle, mocking undertone in his father's voice.

For the first time, Maya looked at him with interest. "You work in the sciences? What field?"

"Actually, I'm a marine archaeologist. Pops thinks anyone who doesn't operate purely on emotion is a scientist."

"I operate on my gut. That's different from emotion," Doc said.

Matt grinned wickedly. "Sure it is, Pops."

Maya smirked. "My dad is the same way," she whispered. "He says he's all about 'evidence' but he only believes evidence that supports what he already believes. Anything that contradicts what his 'instincts' tell him is true is automatically suspect or part of a conspiracy theory."

"What do you know? We already have something in common." They clinked bottles and Matt took a long drink. "What about you? What do you do with yourself when you're not blowing holes in extinct animals?" He hadn't meant to sound so coarse, but Maya didn't appear to have heard him. Her attention was focused on the man who had just entered.

"Good afternoon. I am pleased to see you are all settling in." The speaker was a tall, handsome fellow with perfectly coiffed black hair, a neatly trimmed mustache, and straight, white teeth. He was the very image of the wealthy Spaniard who filled the role of villain in old episodes of Zorro. "I am Santiago Aquino, special attaché from the government of Mexico, tasked with overseeing this very special island."

"When do we get started?" Barnard piped up.

Aquino flashed an indulgent smile, unruffled. "Very soon. But first, there is business to which we must attend. You all signed non-disclosure agreements prior to your arrival. I must caution you that the government takes these very seriously. More importantly, among the few who know about this place, there are some who believe the agreements are not sufficient." He paused to let that sink in.

"What are you telling us?" Maya asked.

Aquino frowned, considering the question. Matt figured it was an act. Aquino probably delivered this same speech to every group of hunters.

"If you should violate our agreement, it is probable that steps will be taken, not by the government and certainly not by me, to silence you permanently. Sadly, our nation has no shortage of capable men and women who would perform that task in exchange for modest compensation." The members of the hunting party exchanged frowns and Aquino held up a hand. "I am not threatening you. I am merely warning you that if you should violate your NDA, we cannot guarantee your safety. So, it would be best if you simply lived up to your word and kept to the terms of our agreement, yes?" He flashed his too-white smile.

"I guess we have no choice," Albert said. "Not that we weren't going to abide by our agreement."

"We're all professionals here." Doc glanced at Matt as he spoke. "We understand the importance of confidentiality. We're just here for the hunt."

"I expected no less from gentlemen..." Aquino paused, "and ladies of your standing." He winked at Maya.

Matt decided this was as good a time as any to ask the foremost of his many questions. "If I may ask, how is this possible? Cloning?"

Aquino shook his head. "It is actually much simpler than that. The Chicxulub impact wiped out almost all of the dinosaurs, but a few survived."

"How?" Matt pressed. The asteroid that had struck the Yucatán Peninsula nearly sixty-six million years ago, forming the Chicxulub Crater, had such a devastating impact that it caused the mass extinction of dinosaurs all around the world. "The island is so close to ground zero."

"That, we do not know. I can only tell you that the fossil record shows the continuous survival of a few species of dinosaurs."

"What kinds of dinos do you have?" Kevin asked.

"I will show you." He nodded at a television hanging on the far wall. As they all turned to look at it, he picked up a remote and clicked. The screen came to life, the video feed flashed to a pair of squat, armored dinosaurs who stood at the edge of a stream, munching on thick grasses. "Ankylosaurus. I do not recommend shooting at them. You will only provoke them."

"Is this a live feed?" Maya asked.

"Recorded footage." Another click. A small herd of bipedal dinosaurs moved across a clearing. Colorful feathers dotted their tough hides.

Matt recognized them immediately. "Hadrosaurs?"

"Correct."

"I still can't believe it," Maya said softly. "They really did have feathers."

"They have much in common with birds, as some famed archaeologists have theorized," Aquino said.

Next came triceratops, followed by a few species with which Matt was not familiar. Most bore a strong resemblance to more familiar dinos, but with minor differences that merited new names. Just as Aquino turned away from the screen, Matt saw something flash across the corner of the screen. He couldn't be certain, but it looked to be the size and shape of a Compsognathus, a scavenger dinosaur that grew to approximately the size of a turkey. The thin veneer of colorful feathers only added to the mental association.

"These are the creatures you are most likely to encounter," Aquino said. "A few species, those that are in need of protection due to their limited numbers, are kept on the north end of the island. That section is off-limits for the protection of the animals. Guests are not to enter that part of the island."

Aquino tapped a button and a map of Bermeja appeared on the screen. The island resembled an elongated skull, the north end large and round, twin lakes forming the eye sockets. The lodge where they now sat was located just south of the lakes. Aquino zoomed in on the south end of the island.

"The animals in this part of the island are not

restricted in their movements, save for the moats that keep them away from the lodge. They tend to keep to themselves. If you wish to hunt different species, you will most likely have to cover the entirety of the Southern Reach, which is what we call this section of Bermeja."

"How much extra will we have to pay in order to bring a trophy home?" Barnard asked.

Aquino turned a tight-lipped smile on the young man. "I am afraid that is impossible, for security reasons."

"Come on. Everybody has a price," Barnard said. "Name it and my father will pay it."

"I fear the price would be one you would not wish to pay. I cannot emphasize enough how seriously this island's security is taken." Aquino's smile was tight and cold. "Although you cannot take trophies, your kills will, of course, be prepared and served at the end-of-hunt banquet

"What does dinosaur taste like?" Maya asked.

"It depends on the animal, but most of them taste like chicken."

Everyone laughed. Everyone except Barnard, who still wanted to take home a prize.

"Surely there's a way we can take something home. A skull, maybe?" Barnard pressed.

"No," Aquino said flatly.

Matt frowned at the map. Something was bothering him. "I don't see any predators among your dinosaur population."

"You are correct. Despite our best efforts, the last carnivores died off. That is why hunting expeditions like these help keep things in balance. We could cull the herd ourselves, of course, but the hunting program funds schools and clinics in the poorest villages in Mexico."

"I assume there are limits on what and how many we can bring down?" Doc asked.

"Mister Tomlin will guide you in that respect. While you are on the hunt, his word is law." Aquino looked at each hunter in turn, his gaze lingering on Barnard, whose face turned scarlet.

"Finally, I must warn you that, although you are here to hunt dinosaurs, those are not the only animals you are likely to encounter. The island is home to poisonous reptiles and other native species which can pose a danger to you. Never think you are safe merely because there are no dinosaurs about." A contemplative silence fell over the group. Aquino bade them goodbye and left the room.

Matt's gaze lingered on the screen, where a single dinosaur stood, looking out at the horizon. As Matt watched, the creature turned toward the camera and Matt thought he saw intelligence there, awareness. His breath caught in his throat. What had he gotten himself into?

End of the road," Tomlin proclaimed, parking the Jeep at the end of a paved road. "We hoof it from here."

The group piled out, Barnard leading the way. He moved a few paces into the forest and swung his rifle to and fro, as if he expected to make a kill right then and there.

"You won't find anything this close to the road," Tomlin said, shouldering an overstuffed pack. "It'll be at least an hour, depending on where the herds are."

"An hour?" Barnard whirled around to face the guide. "What the hell?" he snapped as Matt grabbed the barrel of the young man's rifle and forced it straight up.

"Get your finger off the trigger," Matt said through gritted teeth.

Barnard's face turned scarlet and he moved his finger outside the trigger guard. "I know what I'm doing."

"You'll stay up front with me," Tomlin told Barnard. "Where I can keep an eye on you."

Barnard stiffened, but wilted under the hunting guide's glare. "Whatever. Let's get going."

An hour later, they found themselves kneeling in the midst of a thick stand of palmetto, peering out at a trio of dinosaurs in the distance. The massive bony frills on their heads resembled that of triceratops, but they lacked the long horns.

"They're a variety of ceratopsian," Tomlin said. "Like the trike, but they have stubby horns." He flashed a wolfish grin. "They're nasty sons of bitches. Difficult to kill. Impossible at this range."

He handed Matt a pair of binoculars. Matt zoomed in and focused. The binoculars lent the image a surreal quality, yet he still felt overwhelmed. The powerful creatures moved with a surprising grace for their size. Their flanks heaved with each breath, muscles rippling beneath thick hide and a dusting of silvery gray feathers. Magnificent!

"It feels wrong to kill these beauties," Matt said.

"I felt the same way at first," Tomlin said "But I promise you, we've got a thriving population and the herd has to be culled. On Bermejo, hunting a dino is like hunting a deer back in the states. Without predators here, hunting is an ecological necessity."

"You've hunted these before?" Doc whispered.

Tomlin nodded. "You've got to get up close and get a

perfect shot, just behind the left foreleg, up high where the heart is. If you miss, you'd better put a lot of lead in the air, because it will come for you."

"I'm guessing we're too far away to risk a shot," Matt said. A former Army Ranger, he believed he could make the shot but doubted any of the others could.

"You guessed right," Tomlin said. "A skilled marksman might could do it, but it's not worth the risk."

A shot rang out, deafening in the stillness of the afternoon. Peering through binoculars, Matt had an up-close view of the impact as the bullet glanced off the armor plating of the largest dino. Blood and feathers flew. It let out a bellow, turned, and charged in their direction.

"What in the hell?" Tomlin ripped the rifle away from Barnard, who was already taking aim for another shot. "There's a ledge about fifty meters that way!" He pointed to the west. "Everybody run for it."

The hunters ran as fast as they dared in the dense tropical forest. Matt fell back to the rear, thinking to protect the others. He doubted there was anything he could do that Tomlin couldn't do as well, maybe better, but taking responsibility for his team had been drilled into him over the years beginning with his enlistment. By contrast, Kevin had adopted the "every man for himself" approach. Matt's brother had sprinted well ahead of the party, and was now scaling the rock wall.

Behind them, Matt heard the thunder of heavy feet pounding the soft turf, the angry bellow of the charging beast.

And then it ended.

"She broke off the charge," Tomlin said, looking around. He barely sounded winded despite the sprint through the woods.

"How do you know it's female?" Matt asked, the science teacher in him coming to the fore.

"Just speculating because of her protective behavior. I'm not gonna lift her skirt and find out." He turned and called out to Kevin, who had just reached the top of the ledge. "You can come down from your perch now, little bird."

Kevin paused to catch his breath before climbing down. When he returned to the group, his sheepish expression spoke volumes.

"Sorry, I didn't realize how slow the rest of you are." He winked at Maya, who turned and walked away. "Bitch," he muttered softly enough that only Matt heard. It was a good thing, too, because her father, Albert, looked like he could take Kevin apart with ease.

"Watch your mouth," Matt said. "She doesn't deserve that."

"Or what?" Kevin asked.

"Or I'll close it for you, big brother." Matt bared his teeth in a wolfish grin that Bones would have been proud of.

Kevin paled. "Looks like somebody's in love," he said lamely and turned away.

"Can I have my gun back, now?" Barnard stood, hands on hips. He wore a pith helmet, crisp khakis, and an olive green shirt. He had, of course, popped the collar. He looked absurd.

"Repeat after me. This is my weapon," Tomlin held up Barnard's rifle, "and this is my gun." He pointed the rifle at the young man's crotch.

Albert chimed in. "This is for killing," he flourished his own weapon, "and this is for fun."

Tomlin winked and turned to Barnard. "To answer

your question, no, you may not have your weapon back until I'm satisfied you can follow instructions."

Barnard clenched his fists, cocked his elbows, and then relaxed. In the first display of intelligence Matt had seen from the young man, he exhaled slowly, his posture relaxing. "Sorry."

Tomlin nodded. "Don't let it happen again."

Matt awoke with a start. He rolled over and pressed a hand to his churning stomach. They'd enjoyed a productive hunt and had feasted on choice cuts of the hadrosaur he'd taken. They'd washed it down with a few too many Noche Buena, a rich, dark lager. Now he was paying the price.

"What was that sound?" Maya whispered. She lay a few feet from him, her face illumined by an orange glow.

It only took a moment for him to identify the source of the light. In the distance, the sky glowed, smoke roiling. Now he remembered what had awakened him. It wasn't his stomach, but a loud boom.

Maya seized his hand. "What happened?"

"An explosion. I think it's the lodge."

Voices cut through the darkness; Doc and Albert grumbling muzzy variations on the theme of, "What the hell is going on?"

Matt looked around for Tomlin. "Tomlin, anything on the radio?"

No reply.

A flashlight clicked on, its intense beam slicing through the darkness. Doc strode forward and let out a curse when the light fell on Tomlin. "The man appeared to be asleep, but the gaping wound in his throat and the blood soaking his sleeping bag told a different story.

Maya let out a gasp and covered her mouth. Doc took a step toward the body but Matt grabbed him by the arm.

"Let me. I know what I'm doing." Taking the flashlight from his father's hand, he circled the body, inspecting the ground. He quickly found what he was looking for.

"Footprints. Someone walked right up to him, did the deed, and then headed into the forest in the direction of the lodge." He moved the circle of light along the path the presumed killer had taken.

"What are you, an Indian scout?" Maya asked.

Matt shook his head. "I spend a lot of time in the field and I learned from one of the best."

"You said someone, not something," Doc said. "So, it's not a dinosaur?"

"Does that look like a dinosaur print to you?" Matt shone his light on a partial bootprint.

"Who would have done this?" Maya asked.

Albert piped up. "Barnard or Kevin. They're both missing."

Doc and Maya reacted with surprise, but Matt was distracted by movement in the underbrush. A dark shape scurried out into the light, resolving into the form of a small, feathered dinosaur the size of a chicken. Compys! Two more followed in its wake. They scurried over to where Tomlin's body lay. The largest of the three gave the man a sniff. A long tongue flicked out, tasting the blood. Its head flicked to the side, birdlike, and it let out a chirp. The two smaller dinos answered, then the three began tearing at Tomlin's ruined throat.

Behind him, Matt heard his father lose most of last night's meal. Maya grabbed her rifle, intent on shooting the scavengers.

"There's no point," Matt said. "There are bound to be more of them, and we can't take his body with us when we go. Besides, a shot might alert whatever else is out there."

"Like what?" Albert asked.

"These are scavengers that feed on carcasses. Ask yourself, if the animal population is strictly controlled, select creatures regularly harvested, what is out here for them to feed on?"

"Other animals die out here, don't they?" Doc asked.

Matt nodded but remained unconvinced. "Maybe that's it."

"Maybe they came from the north side of the island?" Maya asked.

"The north end? The part that's off-limits," Albert said.

"Maybe when the lodge blew, it opened the gates that held them in," Maya said.

Doc scratched his chin. "Seems like they'd have redundant systems, failsafes. Shouldn't take a chance, I suppose." He let out a long sigh, deflating. "I'm sorry, son. I truly thought this would be an adventure."

"It definitely is," Matt said. "Let's find Kevin and then we'll make our way to the docks and get the hell out of here." He picked up his rifle and ammunition and followed the footprints into the forest. The others followed his lead, grabbing their weapons and falling in behind him.

About twenty meters away, a second pair of footprints joined those they followed. Out of the corner of his eye, he saw Maya flash a concerned look at him. There was no need to reply. They all knew what it meant—Kevin and Barnard were working together. And considering the comparative sizes of the prints, he was almost certain it had been Kevin who murdered Tomlin.

"What the hell are they up to?" he whispered.

"I'm sorry," Maya said. "It's not easy finding out a family member is an asshole."

Matt didn't reply. Given his family's business dealings, it was not surprising to learn that Kevin was capable of murder, but it was disappointing.

She glanced back at her father. "I've hated that man for as long as I can remember."

"Why are you here, anyway?" Matt said, his tone harsher than he intended.

Maya was silent for a long while. "I work for a non-profit. Dad pays me a generous stipend on the condition that I come home for major holidays and I spend one week pretending we're a happy family. I would tell him to stuff it, but…"

She didn't get the chance to finish. At Matt's four o'clock, something crashed through the undergrowth. He whirled about in time to see a large theropod charge them. It was a good five meters from the point of its snout to the tip of its tail. It stood on two powerful hind legs. A triple line of bony protrusions ran from the base of its skull down along its spine and tail. They jutted up from a blanket of thin, mottled green feathers. Thick patches of black feathers ringed its eyes like a mask. A bladelike horn thrust up from its snout, and two smaller horns jutted out above its eyes. Teeth like daggers gleamed in the dim light.

Even as he raised his rifle, he remembered its name. Ceratosaurus.

Doc stood directly between Matt and the dino,

blocking his line of fire. Before Matt could draw a bead on the dinosaur, it attacked. Moving with surprising speed, it struck at Albert, its powerful jaws slicing off the man's right arm.

Albert screamed as blood spurted from his ruined arm. His rifle clattered to the ground, hand still gripping it. He reeled backwards, gouts of blood spraying in a circle like a lawn sprinkler.

Matt squeezed off a round, but the ceratosaur lowered its head, bobbing birdlike, and bit deeply into Albert's gut, tearing out a mouthful of vital organs. Intestines dangled from the corners of its mouth like spaghetti noodles. Doc, spewing invective, opened up with a wild burst of gunfire. Most of the bullets went wide, but a few found their marks.

The ceratosaur, its jaws still clamped around a mouthful of Texan, let out a shriek and fled into the undergrowth. Doc, roaring incoherently, chased it with a stream of bullets.

"Pops! You're wasting ammo!"

The sound of Matt's voice got Doc's attention. "Right." Breathing heavily, he turned to Maya, who stood motionless, eyes locked on what remained of her father. "I'm so sorry about your dad."

"It's okay." She knelt beside the body, reached into a pocket, and drew out an old Zippo lighter. She flicked it on and held it close to Albert's head, bathing his face in a circle of flickering light. "He was awful in a lot of ways but he was my dad."

Matt didn't know what to say, so he turned and led them through the forest. In the distance they heard shouts and bursts of gunfire.

"Is that Kevin and Barnard?" Maya asked.

Matt shook his head. "Too many voices. Got to be security." He returned to tracking. An occasional footprint was enough to tell Matt that both Barnard and Kevin had come this way. For what reason, he still didn't know.

"Matt," Maya said, "I think we're being followed."

Matt looked back just in time to catch a glimpse of a dark shape moving toward them. He glimpsed its feather-flecked hide, caught a glint of firelight reflected in its eyes.

"I got this. You two watch our flanks!"

The last three words were drowned in a torrent of gunfire as another ceratosaur charged them and the three hunters opened fire. Bullets tore into its tough hide, pinged its thick skull. Matt took careful aim at the spot where he thought its heart would be and fired.

The dinosaur let out a shriek. Blood and feathers flew. It slowed its pace, but kept coming, the hunters retreating before its charge.

"It's not dying!" Maya shouted.

And then it fell in a heap.

Relief tinged with regret at killing such a magnificent creature flooded through Matt.

Doc turned to him and grinned. "Well, that was… Aaaah!" He let out a bloodcurdling cry as, with viperlike quickness, a head popped out of the forest cover and bit him just below the rib cage. He fell to the ground, still screaming.

Matt fired at the creature that was already tensed to spring again. A hail of bullets, and then his weapon ran dry. It was enough. The dinosaur, a juvenile ceratosaur, lay twitching in a pool of blood that was already soaking into the soft earth.

"Keep watch," he told Maya, then turned and knelt

beside his father.

It was a grisly sight. Blood poured from the deep, ragged wound. He knew immediately it would prove fatal. Still, he began stripping off his shirt.

"Hang on, Pops. I'm going to bandage you up."

"Stop," Doc rasped.

"I'm going to take care of you." He was proud that his tone betrayed neither the certainty of his father's imminent demise, nor the regret he felt at never having bridged the gap between them.

"Listen," Doc said with surprising force. "No time. I'm already dead. My body just hasn't figured it out."

A sudden surge of regret pinched the back of Matt's throat and his eyes misted. "All right."

"I'm leaving the company to you. Kevin… no imagination… doesn't think deeply… a yes man. A schemer."

"Pops, I can't do what you guys do. I'm not that person."

"You'll figure it out." Doc shuddered as a wave of pain surged through him. "The portals," he gasped. "Don't let him…" His eyes closed.

"Wake up, Pops! What portals?"

Doc stared up at the sky through lifeless eyes.

Matt couldn't begin to wrap his head around what his father had told him. The company was… his? And something about portals? He felt Maya grip his shoulder.

"Come on," she said gently. "We've got to go."

"We're not going that way." Matt peered down a gentle

slope toward the docks. A half-dozen velociraptors barred their way. They milled about, occasionally snapping at one another, but never straying far from the shore.

"It's almost like they're standing guard," Maya said. "What do we do?"

Matt shrugged. "Work our way north and then follow the shoreline down."

Maya smirked. "I hope dinosaurs can't swim."

Going north required passing the lodge, which necessitated crossing the moats that bisected the island. When they reached the bridge that spanned the first moat, Matt was pleased to see it had not been damaged by the explosion. He looked around to make sure no dinosaurs were about, then reached out to take Maya by the hand.

"What are you doing? I can walk just fine by myself."

"Oh, sorry."

"Here, make yourself useful." She shoved her rifle into his hands. "I've seen you shoot. You're better than me." She grimaced at the admission. "Only a few bullets left in the magazine, so make them count."

It didn't take long for Matt to exhaust the remaining rounds. No sooner had Maya stepped out onto the bridge than a dark shadow swooped down upon her. Matt fired instinctively, ripping through the creature and sending it tumbling down into the moat.

"What the hell?" Maya pressed her hands to the top of her head as if checking to make sure everything was still there.

"Pterodactyl," Matt said. Down at the bottom of the deep concrete moat, the body of the flying reptile was easy to spot. "But that makes no sense. How could they keep flying creatures on the island?"

"They didn't keep them on the island," a voice said.

"That thing came through the portal."

Barnard stepped out onto the bridge, blocking their path. Gone was the petulant trust fund kid. Now he moved with a calm, self-assuredness. His grin was that of a predator.

"What's going on?" Matt said. He and Maya backed away from the bridge. "Where's my brother?"

"Looking for the portal. I think he plans on going through."

"What portal?" Maya asked.

"Haven't you figured it out?" Barnard sneered. "The dinosaurs are not survivors from the Late Jurassic or whenever the hell they were supposed to have lived here. They come here through a portal that connects our world to another one."

"Like a time portal?" Maya asked.

Barnard shrugged. "I don't know if it connects to another time or another world. What I can tell you is it is only active certain times of the year, and the Mexicans have a way of controlling it during that time. I think it's some kind of wormhole."

"That's nuts!" Maya said.

"Wormholes are theoretically possible," Matt said. He'd heard enough lectures from Bones and their crewmate Corey Dean to last a lifetime. Insane as Bernard's words sounded, Matt believed him.

Maya gaped at him. "You aren't taking this seriously, are you?"

"Trust me. I've seen crazier." He looked to Barnard. "Any idea how they control the portal?"

Barnard laughed. "All I know is their cover story. They claim several years back the US government came into possession of a trove of Atlantean artifacts. In typical government fashion, the artifacts were 'misplaced' and someone on the inside has been selling them. I can believe it except for the Atlantean part."

Matt felt cold all over. A wave of nausea churned inside his gut and he felt dizzy. He knew where the Atlantean artifacts came from."

"Your father knew," Barnard said to Matt. "Where are he and Albert? Dead? If so, that would save me some trouble."

"Why are you doing this?" Maya asked.

"Kevin's obsessed. He tried to access your father's files on portals, but he's locked out. Apparently, your dear old dad didn't trust him."

Matt didn't miss the fact that, like Doc, Barnard had said "portals" plural.

"What kind of business is your family in?" Maya asked.

"Grocery stores," Matt said. "And firearms, weed, and money laundering."

"And wormholes?" she asked.

"Apparently." Matt turned to Barnard. "And what's your reason for getting involved in all of this?"

"Me? My motivation is simple. Revenge." He didn't wait for them to ask him to elaborate. "The woman I loved came here on a hunting trip with her old man. She came back in a closed casket. But I opened it." He shivered. "So, to paraphrase David Keith, I'm 'burning it all down, baby.'" He flashed a wicked smile, eyes wide and gleaming maniacally.

"That's got nothing to do with us," Maya said. "We just want to get out of here."

Barnard made a clucking sound and waggled his finger. "Sorry, but you know too much. I do want to have a life when I get back. So, I'm afraid I'll have to dispose of all witnesses."

Matt knew this was the moment. When Barnard reached for the pistol tucked in his waistband, Matt flung the empty rifle in the man's direction and charged. Barnard dodged the flying weapon and managed to get his pistol clear of its holster but couldn't take aim before Matt seized his wrist.

Matt was the larger man, but Barnard was surprisingly strong and agile. He twisted and nearly managed to tip Matt off-balance, but Matt held on and drove the lighter man backward like a football player hitting a blocking sled. Barnard head butted Matt across the bridge of the nose. Pain blossomed in his face and wetness poured from his nostrils, but Matt kept pushing Barnard inexorably back over the bridge and toward the burning building.

Barnard realized what was happening when the heat became unbearable. He shifted his weight and tried again to throw Matt off-balance, but Matt had plenty of practice at this sort of thing, not to mention extensive training in hand-to-hand combat. When Barnard twisted, Matt used the motion against his opponent. He slammed Barnard's gun hand against a burning section of wall. Barnard let out a cry of pain and rage, dropped his pistol, and somehow managed to break free.

Matt turned to meet his attack, but Barnard was fast. He snapped off a roundhouse kick that caught Matt in the knee and followed with a sharp jab to Matt's broken nose.

Matt blinked away the pain in time to see Barnard shift his feet and drive a sidekick at Matt's midsection. He had expected the attack. Barnard wasn't strong enough to force Matt bodily into the fire, but a well-placed kick could do the job. He pivoted, and the kick struck him a glancing blow. He caught Barnard's leg, held on, and drove forward, this time pushing the younger man away from the fire.

Barnard struggled to remain on his feet, or foot, as things now stood. He didn't realize what Matt was doing until it was too late.

"What! No! Noooo!" His arms flailed, hands snapping closed as if grasping an invisible rope, and he plunged into the moat. When he struck bottom, he didn't rise again.

"Nice job," Maya said. "I would have helped you out, but I figured you had it under control."

"Thanks. Now let's get the hell out of here."

Between the spreading fire and the dinosaurs that roamed the island, making their way to the shore proved to be almost impossible. They soon found themselves hiding in a maintenance shed as a familiar sight strode past them.

"Was that a T-Rex?" Maya whispered.

Matt nodded. "Remember, they track movement, so wait until it's well out of sight before we go."

"Trust me; I couldn't move right now if I wanted to."

Matt waited until he was certain the apex predator was gone, and then he peeked around the corner of the shed. In the darkness, he caught sight of a flickering blue light. It came from a cave set in a low hillock. A massive security gate stood open beside it.

"That's the portal. It's got to be," he whispered. As if

to confirm his suspicion, a velociraptor sprinted out of the cave and off into the darkness.

"Who cares? Let's go."

"We should close it. Permanently."

Maya fixed him with a flat stare. "I don't know whether to begin with 'why' or 'how.' Dealer's choice."

Matt frowned. He couldn't explain it, but deep down he knew he ought to close off access to the portal. Besides, if Barnard's story was true, Matt was partially responsible for all of this. "Whatever Kevin wants with it, it can't be good. He's not the ethical type. Besides, the fewer dinosaurs out here stalking us, the better."

"Okay, let's move along to the 'how' of the situation. I don't see any kind of control mechanism."

"I want to destroy the portal itself. We've got all the makings for a nice bomb right here in the shed." His sweeping gesture took in several bags of fertilizer and a variety of other items.

"You know how to do that? From your time in the service?"

"That and a basic knowledge of chemistry. Let's go."

Thirty minutes later they stood at the mouth of the cave, ready to set off the bomb. Matt had not had time to inspect the portal, except to ascertain that there were no controls anywhere in the vicinity. If they were using alien tech to control this, they were doing it from a remote location, and he had no idea where to look for it.

A blue glow emanated from the bedrock. He saw tiny flecks of blue scattered across the surface of the stone.

Some sort of crystal or previously-unknown mineral, perhaps? He wouldn't figure it out standing here. He needed to blow this thing before something hungry stepped through and made him a midnight snack.

"You think it will work?" Maya asked.

"No idea if it will destroy the portal, but it should collapse the passageway. Now, get as far away as you can." He took hold of the wires that would detonate the bomb, and knelt, ready to touch them to the battery he'd scavenged from a four-wheeler.

"Don't do that, brother." Kevin's voice rang out in the semi-darkness. "If your hand moves toward that battery, I kill the girl."

Matt froze. Did he dare try and set off the bomb, trusting that the blast would distract Kevin long enough for Maya to get away?

"Kevin, why the hell are you doing this?"

Light from the dying fire at the lodge danced on Kevin's sweaty brow. He looked like the devil. "Making my own way, little brother. Dad's not going to leave me the company."

"You can have the company," Matt said. "I will sign it over to you. Just get a grip."

"My dreams are bigger than that. I'm going to find and take control of the portals."

"Why? What is the deal with these portals? What do you even want with them?"

Kevin shook his head. "I'd explain it to your dumb ass but I don't see the point. You're both going to be dead in a moment. Now, slowly put the wires down, or I shoot her in the gut so she'll die slowly and painfully. I promise I'll let you live long enough to hear every last one of her screams."

Matt laid the wires on the damp ground, scanning the area with his peripheral vision, searching for a weapon. Nothing.

"Good. Now go stand beside your girlfriend."

Matt did as instructed, glaring at Kevin all the while. "Why don't you put that gun down and fight me like a man? Don't be a little bitch."

Kevin flinched. His buttons were easy to push. He lowered his pistol for a fraction of a second. Matt took a few steps toward him, but Kevin raised his weapon again.

"Nice try. You might be smarter but I'm more clever."

"Cleverer," Matt corrected.

Again, Kevin flinched. Nobody liked having their grammar corrected, but Kevin hated it.

"Correct me again and I'll shoot her just for fun."

Matt tensed. He could see only one option. He'd charge Kevin, probably get shot, but it would give Maya a chance to get away.

"Not yet." Maya's soft whisper scarcely reached his ears. He froze. "If you're going to unlock the portal," she said to Kevin, "you'll need the key."

Kevin frowned. "What key is that?"

"The one I stole from Aquino's office. You see, my dad and I knew about the portals, too."

"Are you kidding me?" Matt couldn't believe his ears.

Maya kept her attention focused on Kevin. "It's in my pocket. I'll give it to you, but you have to let us go."

"Let me see what it is and I'll consider it." Kevin sounded doubtful.

Everything seemed to happen at once. There was a click, then a light blossomed over Matt's shoulder. It arced through the air and landed at Kevin's feet. Matt recognized Albert's Zippo lighter.

A roar sounded in the darkness and something massive came crashing out of the forest. The T-Rex!

Drawn by the light and movement from the Zippo, it charged straight at Kevin. Matt saw a flash of razor sharp teeth and then the jaws closed around Kevin's abdomen. Kevin screamed as he was lifted high, and emptied his pistol into dinosaur's tough hide. The T-Rex let out a muffled roar and dashed back into the cave, carrying Kevin along like a dog with a bone.

"Let's go!" Maya shouted.

"Not yet." Matt returned to his makeshift detonator, grabbed the wires, and touched them to the battery terminals.

The world erupted in fire and smoke.

Matt opened his eyes to see the gray morning sky hanging above him. A gentle rocking and low hum told him he was lying on the deck of a boat. He made to rise, but a stabbing pain in his head sent him back to the deck, groaning.

"You're awake." Maya's face appeared above him, grinning.

"I take it the bomb worked." His voice sounded odd, then he remembered his nose, broken in the fight with Barnard.

"You collapsed the cave, but a chunk of flying rock caught you on the head." She held up a piece of rock the size of his fist. "I saved it for you. A souvenir."

"Thanks." Once again, his eyes were drawn to the blue flecks in the stone. He would have to have it analyzed.

"You're lucky to be alive," Maya said.

"Lucky. That's me." He squeezed his eyes shut and took a few deep breaths. "How'd you get me to the boat?"

"A couple of security guys found us. We're finally getting off this cursed island."

Matt made another attempt at sitting up, and this time managed it. He felt Maya snake her arm around his waist, and he returned the gesture.

"There's something I've been wondering. Your dad left you the family business, which, according to you, is a front for organized crime. Does that make you Tony Soprano?"

Matt considered the question. He was now owner of Barnaby Foods. At least, he would be when all the legalities were settled, and that was going to open a whole new can of worms. Just thinking of it made his head hurt.

"I have no idea what to do about it. If I go to the authorities, I risk implicating the people I love the most. But I really don't want to be in business with shady characters. I keep my life simple."

"What you need is someone who lives in the gray area of society and who knows how to navigate those waters," Maya said.

Matt sat up straight. He knew exactly who to call. "Like a casino owner!"

Maya quirked an eyebrow. "You sound like you have somebody in mind."

Matt pulled her close. "Oh, I do. Let me tell you a story about my friend's uncle, Crazy Charlie."

DARK ENTRY

While searching for a lost Native American artifact, Maddock and Bones run afoul of some locals who are playing a very dangerous game.

This short story originally appeared in *The Game* anthology published by Seven Realms publishing. It was later rewritten and incorporated in the Dane Maddock novel *Ark*. It is published here in its original form.

DARK ENTRY

"This looks like the place."

Bones glanced at the weathered sign. Despite the faded letters, he could make out the words National Park Service, Black Break, Virginia. The condition of the office building was not much better. The brown paint was peeling off in patches the size of swim fins and seedling pines peeked over the edge of the gutter that ran along the front of the single-story building.

"Not too impressed, I have to say." Dane Maddock shook his head as he took in the sight. "Definitely not ship-shape."

"It's not an episode of Cribs," Bones said. "I just need directions to the battlefield. You can wait here. It should only take a minute." He left the car running so Maddock could keep listening to Bruce Springsteen.

He bypassed the sagging stairs and stepped directly up onto the covered porch. A solitary rocking chair sat by the screen door. A discarded newspaper lay alongside it beneath a JFG coffee can that had obviously been put to use as a spittoon. Bones wrinkled his nose and drew the door open. The hinges, much in need of oil, announced his arrival before he could step inside.

A wrinkled woman stood behind the counter, watching The Price is Right on a tiny color television. She wore a crisp tan uniform, with a tag that named her Betty Tull. She initially spared him only a glance as he entered, then snapped her head around and gaped at him.

"I know," he said with a grin. "I'm the tallest Indian you've ever seen." A six foot-four Cherokee was not a common sight in any neck of the woods.

"You've heard that before, I reckon?" She kept staring at him, not the least bit embarrassed by her reaction of moments before.

"A time or two. I was wondering if you could give me directions..." The sudden change in Betty's expression made him pause. Her eyes narrowed to slits, her lips pursed, and she directed her full attention to the door behind him. He spun around, his hand instinctively going to his hip where he had worn a sidearm for so many years in the service, and still wore it on occasion, but no one was there.

"Did you sit in that rocking chair, young man?" She sounded like a teacher scolding her pupil. He shook his head. "It's moving. Did you push it? Brush against it?"

"No Ma'am. Why? Is it an antique?"

"A bad omen," she muttered. She bit her lip, then returned her attention to Bones. "Anyhow, you were saying?"

"I was hoping you could give me directions. I understand there's a Civil War battlefield in this area."

"The battlefield." It was as if a shade had been drawn down across her face, all previous emotion gone.

"Yes. One of my ancestors fought in a battle somewhere near here back during the war. I was hoping to visit the site. Maybe take a few pictures." He gave her a congenial smile and leaned casually against the counter, trying to put her at ease.

"I'll help the gentleman, Betty." A keg of a man almost bursting out of his park ranger uniform stepped out from a door behind the counter. "You can go on and take your lunch break." He smiled at Bones and offered his hand. "I'm Earl Eddings, the ranger in these parts."

"Bones." He shook the ranger's strong, calloused

hand. Clearly this Eddings fellow did more than sit behind a desk all day. "That's what they call me, anyway. My mother stuck me with a weird name."

"Understood." Eddings grinned. "So, you say you're looking for Dark Entry?"

"I'm looking for the site of the Battle of Stonesburg. Is that the same place?"

"Stonesburg's the Yankee name for it. They won the war, so..." He shrugged. "Dark Entry is the name of the stream that feeds the lake at the site of the battle. You can't properly call it a battlefield, since it was more of a skirmish in a mountain valley, but it's all we've got around here."

Bones' heart beat faster. So at least that part of the story was accurate, and if that part was true, why not the rest?

"Are you going to tell him about the curse?" Betty leaned through the doorway. "It's only right. You can't let him go up there and have Lord knows what happen to him."

"I will tell him. Thank you, Betty." Eddings kept his voice pleasant, though his eyes were stony. "Sorry about that. It's a remote location, and the site has had its share of tragedies: drownings, fatal falls, hikers gone missing. Couple that with the long-standing belief that the site is haunted, and you can see why some people," he rolled his eyes toward the open office door, "let their superstitious beliefs get the better of them. There's no reason for concern as long as you use caution. Just watch your step, and keep an eye out for the bears and the snakes."

"I'll be careful. Do you have a map that shows how to get there? I'll be happy to pay for it."

"No, but I'll draw you one. It's not too difficult." Eddings took out a legal pad, tore off the faded top page, and sketched out a map. He jotted a few notes about landmarks and emphasized what he said were the more confusing turns. When he finished, he passed the paper to Bones. "You taking anyone up there with you?"

There was something about the too-casual way in which the Ranger asked the question that told Bones he should not answer truthfully. "Nope. Just me." For an instant, he feared the ranger was about to offer to accompany him, which would be entirely out of the question, considering what Bones and Maddock planned to do. "It's kind of a personal journey for me. Trying to get in touch with the spirit of my ancestor, you know."

Eddings' smile did not reach his eyes, but he nodded and assured Bones that he understood completely. That was one of the advantages to being an Indian. You could heap a big, steaming pile of spiritual crap onto someone and they'd believe it every time. He shook Eddings' hand, called a thank-you to Betty, and slipped out the door. This time, he was extra careful to not touch the rocking chair.

"Think this is it?" Maddock took in the narrow valley. Dark pines leaned in on all sides, as if daring anyone to try to climb out. A mountain stream cascaded down moss-covered rocks into a tiny lake of deep green. In the distance, the open field that must have been the site of the battle gave way to a dense forest.

"It fits the description." Bones gazed out across the water. "If the story is true, the cavern should be somewhere in the area of that waterfall." He pointed to the falls.

"So, how did your great, great granduncle come to be fighting for the Confederacy in the first place?"

"Three greats," Bones corrected. "Thanks to the Indian Removal Act, he was raised by a family that despised the federal government. When Jackson sent the soldiers in, my family hid in the mountains. They hated living like refugees in land that was rightfully their own. When the Civil War began, my uncle saw what he thought was a chance to strike a blow of his own. I don't know if he was light-skinned enough to pass or if the Confederates in his area were just desperate enough for fighting men that they didn't much care who enlisted."

Maddock nodded. "So, the story is, by the time he came to this battle, he'd been carrying this family heirloom throughout the war?"

"Yes, but it wasn't just an heirloom. He claimed it was an item of great power. Anyway, when he saw the battle was lost and his company surrounded, he dove into the pond, thinking he could swim away and find a place to hide." Bones moved closer to the water, his eyes locked on the far shore as if he could see right through the mountainside. "He had almost made it to the far shore when the Yankees saw him and started shooting. He dove down as deep as he could and came across the entrance to the underwater cavern. I don't know what possessed him to swim into it, not knowing if there would be air pockets, but he did.

"The cavern led back into the mountainside, but it wasn't long before the way became too narrow for him to keep going. He hid there as long as he could, but he was soaking wet and had no way to get dry or to make a fire, and he also had no food. He hid his treasure in the cave and swam back out to take a look around. If the Yankees were gone, he figured he could retrieve his treasure and try to find his way to safety."

"But it didn't happen that way?"

Bones shook his head. "They caught him almost as soon as he surfaced. They didn't know where he'd been hiding, and didn't much care. They took him prisoner. After the war, he was in no condition to make the trip back in search of what he'd lost. He eventually married, had children, and there was no good time to leave in search of a lost treasure. He wasn't even sure he could find the place again, he remembered so little. It wasn't like today, with maps, the internet, and GPS. Finally, he decided he was too old to make the trip, but he made certain to tell the story and he insisted that it be passed down in the family.

"You should be proud," Maddock said. "Whether we find anything or not, you solved a family mystery. That's a big deal." He fished a quarter from his pocket. "Flip you to see who has to stay topside."

"No need." Bones waved the coin away. "I told the ranger I'd be coming up here alone. I don't know why, but I just had a feeling. Wouldn't surprise me if he showed up to check on us, and if he sees you here with our car, he's going to want to know where I am."

"We can't have that now, can we?" Maddock grinned. In general, he didn't care for freshwater dives, but if the choice was between that or standing around doing nothing for an hour, he'd take the fresh water. In a matter of minutes, he was suited up and ready to dive.

"Don't fart around down there," Bones said. "I'll stick near the shore, look like a tourist, and try to keep an eye out for you. And try not to get tangled. I really don't want to come in after you. Mountain lakes are cold."

"I'm definitely not looking forward to the shrinkage factor." Maddock grimaced.

"How can you tell the difference?" Bones took a quick step back. "Just kidding, bro. Have a good dive." He fished a small camera from his pocket and strolled away. "Oh! By the way!" he called as Maddock stepped into the water. "Don't forget to bring me back a present!"

Maddock gritted his teeth as he waded into the chilly lake. His full suit would keep him fairly warm, but just knowing he was surrounded by all that cold water was enough to raise goose bumps all over his body. He was a Caribbean and Gulf of Mexico kind of guy, not a mountain man. He slipped beneath the dark water, wishing for sun, salt, and a Dos Equis with lime.

The sun's rays did not penetrate more than a few meters below the water's surface, but the beam of his dive light revealed boulders and sunken logs, all coated with decayed vegetation. He swam with care, not wanting to limit visibility by stirring up the debris. A few small fish darted by, but otherwise he saw few signs of life.

Near the waterfall, there was no need to be concerned about stirring up silt. Water roiled and churned, bringing visibility down to a few feet. He had worried that the cave, if it existed, might have already been discovered. Now, seeing the murky cloud someone would have to penetrate, he felt hope rising. He dove down as far as he could, careful to watch for potential snares, and swam hard against the force of the surging water. He kicked harder, creeping inexorably toward his goal.

His hands met stone an instant before his face would have. He found an uneven rock edge and held on tight, his body buffeted by the force of the waterfall. Slowly and methodically, he searched the area below the waterfall.

His gloved hands probed each crevice and recess, but to no avail.

After a few passes, he was on the verge of declaring the cave a myth when his light fell on an odd rock formation just beyond the area he had been searching. Behind an upright stone formation lay a dark, vertical gash in the wall. His heart pounding, he slid behind the rock and into the crevasse. The way was narrow and his shoulders almost touched the sides, but after a few feet, the fissure opened up again and he came to a sheer wall. He changed direction, followed his bubbles upward, until at last he broke the surface inside a pitch black cavern. He had found it!

Bones kept a close eye on the calm, dark lake. He tracked Maddock's progress by the bubbles rising to the otherwise smooth surface of the water until, finally, the turbulence around the waterfall hid all signs of his partner. *Hurry up, Maddock.*

The roar of a vehicle coming up the dirt road caught his ear. The nosy ranger coming to check up on him. Bones turned his camera on and aimed it at the waterfall, trying to look like a sightseer. He'd voiced his concern that the man might show up, so he had every confidence that Maddock would be cautious about his return to the surface.

The roar grew louder and Bones realized that several vehicles were approaching. A keen sense of vulnerability pierced his heart and he suddenly wished he had not left his gun in the car. Abandoning any pretense of casual sightseeing, he hurried back around the edge of the lake toward the place they had parked, but he had not gone more than twenty paces when a pickup barreled out of the woods. The truck shot out onto the grassy valley floor, fishtailed as it turned, and then headed straight for Bones.

An open-top jeep, its driver looking stern, but the fellow in the passenger seat hooting like a hog caller, and two more pickups followed behind. The lead truck skidded to a halt right in front of Bones. The driver gave a friendly wave before climbing out of the cab. The jeep pulled up alongside the truck. The young man on the passenger side was smiling and waving as well.

Bones didn't relax one bit. Rednecks got on his nerves in the best of circumstances, and these circumstances were far from the best. He nodded politely to the first man, a broad-shouldered fellow of early middle years, whose flannel-covered paunch hung down over what Bones just knew was a big silver belt buckle.

The two in the jeep were ruddy-faced and flaxen-haired, clearly father and son. The driver's face was lined and his temples dusted with white. Were it not for the added years, the two could have been brothers, even twins. The hunting rifles they suddenly leveled at Bones, however, were identical.

"Hands behind your head, boy." The paunchy man who had arrived first drew an old Colt long barrel and leveled it at Bones' head. "You got any weapons on you?"

"No, but I'd sure love to shoot that revolver of yours." Though his thoughts were racing a mile a minute, years of training and experience in tight situations kept him calm. "What model?"

"U.S. Army 1903. But I don't let nobody shoot this 'cept me. Do I, Nathan?" The young man in the jeep shook his head. "Tell you what. We'll wait for the others to get here before I search you. You look like you might could give somebody a spot of trouble if you had a mind to."

"Yes, he does, Carter." The driver of the jeep spoke in a deep, rich voice befitting a politician or a morning radio host. "He does indeed."

"Not me," Bones said. "I'm a wuss. I take bubble baths and listen to Kenny what's-his-name. That curly-haired dude."

"Kenny Rogers?" Nathan pursed his lips. "Naw, that Footloose guy. Kenny Loggins!" His face lit up like he'd just guessed the answer to Final Jeopardy.

"He's a funny one," Carter said. Far behind him, the two pickup trucks had boxed in their car, and their passengers had unloaded. There were four of them, all carrying rifles and looking decidedly inbred. Bones soon found himself surrounded by seven hillbillies, all of whom looked like they could handle their weapons.

"You gonna' search him, Carter?" Nathan could not keep a tremor of excitement from his voice. "Search him so we can get started."

Carter silenced Nathan with a glance before holstering his pistol and approaching Bones with cautious steps.

"I'm going to search you, boy. You try anything funny, I promise you'll be dead in the time it takes these fellows to pull the trigger. You understand me?"

Bones nodded. He had no doubt he could kill Carter, and perhaps a second man, but seven was far too many to take on single-handed, and unarmed to boot. Even if Maddock were to show up right now, he had no weapon, and thus would be able to do little, if anything, to help. Bones' best hope was to remain alive and hope Maddock would realize what was going on and come up with a plan. He waited impatiently while Carter patted him down, relieving him of his watch, wallet, keys, and camera.

"Here's how it's going to work." Carter stepped back as he spoke, pocketing Bones' possessions before drawing his pistol again. "You are going to run thataway." He nodded in the direction of the forest. "In five minutes, Kevin here is going to fire his rifle." One of the late arrivals, a moon-faced young man with a wispy mustache and a lip bulging from a wad of chewing tobacco, nodded. "That'll let you know we're coming for you. We want to make it sportsmanlike, you know." Carter grinned.

"What the hell are you talking about?" Bones kept his voice level, but his insides were ice. The man couldn't be serious.

"Just a little game we like to play. It's much more entertaining than deer hunting, and sometimes more challenging." Carter glanced at his wristwatch. "You should get moving. You've already wasted ten seconds."

"And you ain't got that many left to live. Run boy!" Nathan fired off a shot near Bones' feet.

Still unable to believe what was happening, Bones dashed toward the forest, wondering all the while how he was going to get out of this alive.

Maddock shone his light around the cavern. It was very much like Bones had described: a wedge-shaped passage leading back into darkness. He slipped out of his mask, tank, and fins, and began to explore. The walls grew narrower the deeper he went. It was far from the tightest space he had ever been in, but he was well aware of the need for caution. It was all too easy to get stuck in a place like this if one was not careful.

The unyielding stone of the cave was virtually without feature, save the occasional fissure, each of which he inspected with care. The walls closed tighter around him with each step and soon he was forced to turn sideways in order to keep moving. He wondered if Bones' ancestor had been a skinnier man than himself. If so, Maddock might not be able to penetrate deep enough into the cramped passage to find the hiding place.

Finally, the way grew too narrow for him to proceed. He shone his light up and down the walls of unrelenting gray stone. Nothing. He did not want to risk getting stuck, but what if it the hiding place was only a bit farther away? He couldn't go back and tell Bones he had failed unless he was certain the thing was not here. He had to try. He bent his knees, lowering his torso and gaining a bit of space, and squeezed forward one small step, then another. The cold stone pressed into his chest and shoulder blades. Much more of this and he would no longer be able to breathe.

And then he saw it.

Just a few feet ahead, something darker than the natural rock was wedged inside a head-high crack in the wall. He could not switch his flashlight to his right hand, so he held it in his teeth and reached out. His outstretched fingers met smooth stone. He was tantalizingly close-- an inch, if that. He took two shallow breaths, forced all the air from his lungs, relaxed as he exhaled, and slipped deeper down the passageway. Stretching... reaching... until his hand closed around the object and he slid it free.

It was a tomahawk carved from some sort of shiny

black stone he did not immediately recognize and it was surprisingly heavy. A meteorite? He and Bones would give it a closer examination once he got it out into daylight. First, he had to get out of this cave. The tight walls were constricting his chest, making breathing impossible. He was conditioned to holding his breath for extended periods of time, but his body was beginning to complain about the lack of oxygen. He tried to move back toward the entrance, but could not. He was stuck.

Someone with less experience might have panicked in this situation and inadvertently gasped for breath. Maddock remained calm, adjusted his position, and relaxed. With a supreme effort of will, he coaxed the last remnants of air from his lungs, and pushed.

He did not budge an inch.

He continued to lean in his intended direction, careful not to push too hard and wedge himself too tightly to escape. Spots danced in front of his eyes, and his lungs screamed for oxygen. He felt along the wall with his right hand and found a crack into which he was able to work his index and middle fingers. He was unable to bend his elbow in these tight quarters, but he pulled with all the strength he had in his hand. Fire coursed down his arm, and his legs trembled.

After all my close calls, I'm going to die stuck in a freaking tunnel. Thanks, Bones.

And then he moved. It was only a centimeter, if that, but he had definitely moved. His fingers flexed, his chest slid along the cold stone, and then he was free.

With agonizing slowness he continued to move forward, resisting the urge to take a breath and risk getting himself stuck again. It was only a matter of seconds, but it felt like a week before he could fill his lungs with precious oxygen. No longer fearing for his life, he permitted himself a moment to take a closer look at what he had found.

It was definitely a tomahawk, and he thought perhaps it *was* carved from a meteorite. It seemed too substantial for mere stone, yet the substance was not quite metal. A virtual field guide to fauna of the eastern United States was etched all across its surface: bears, cougars, wolves, coyotes, birds of prey, snakes, stags, alligators, even bison, and what looked like a woolly mammoth. He couldn't see anything especially mysterious about it, but it was a fine piece, and Bones would be stoked that they had solved the old family mystery.

Of course, he would have to mess with Bones' head first. Maddock would tell him that rednecks had found the place first and trashed it with Bud Light cans, Marlboro butts, and Copenhagen tins. One of them must have found it first, Bones. Sorry about that. Grinning at the thought of his friend's reaction, he stashed the tomahawk in his mesh dive bag and donned his dive gear.

He had just put the regulator between his teeth and was about to jump into the water when he heard a muffled crack like a gunshot. He paused, straining to make out further sounds above the subdued rush of the waterfall on the other side of the cavern wall, but he heard nothing else. He was sure it had been a gunshot. Water was an excellent conductor of sound. An icy ball formed in the pit of his stomach. He and Bones had stashed their side arms in the car in order to avoid raising unnecessary suspicion should the ranger pay them a visit. What reason would Bones have to retrieve his Glock, much less fire it? Certain he was not going to like what he found outside, he drew his dive knife and slid into the water.

He exited the cavern and surfaced beneath the waterfall. Careful to avoid notice until he knew what was going on, he pushed back his mask and inched out until he could see through the haze.

Seven armed men stood off to the side of the lake, pointing at something in the distance and laughing. Down on the far end, where the dirt road opened onto the battlefield, two pickup trucks had the car blocked in. Something serious was going on.

He weighed his options. He could swim to the far end of the lake, try to slip out unnoticed, and retrieve their weapons from the car. Problem was, Bones had the keys and Maddock had no idea if they had left the vehicle unlocked. He couldn't take out seven armed men with only a knife and in any case, he needed to be completely certain that the men meant the two of them harm. Of course, all signs pointed to that conclusion.

He would have to get closer in order to hear what they were saying without them spotting him. It was easily done, he'd had plenty such training, but in those cases he was outfitted in something less conspicuous than a blue neoprene suit. He dove down deep, staying as close as he dared to the lake bed as he approached his target and then surfaced in silence among the thick reeds at the water's edge.

"Has it been five minutes yet?" a young man asked, tapping his booted foot.

"Hold your horses. It's almost time." The speaker looked like an older, more sober version of the young man. "I want you to stay close to me. This one looks like he might actually give us a challenge." The young man started to object, but the older man talked over him. "This is not deer hunting. A man, even an unarmed one, is an infinitely more dangerous quarry."

Maddock tensed. Was he serious? The pieces fell into place quickly. Bones was alive, unarmed, and in the woods somewhere in the direction in which the men were staring. And these men intended to kill him. The only positive of which Maddock could think was that these yokels didn't seem to know Bones was not alone. What Maddock could do about it remained to be seen.

"I reckon that's long enough." One of the men checked his watch. "Yep. That'll do." He turned to another of his party. "Bevel, it's your turn to guard the vehicles."

"Aww! C'mon Carter." Bevel took off his camouflage NASCAR number three hat and fanned his face. "The kid's the new one in the group. Give him the first shift."

"No. He at least deserves a chance to draw first blood. If we haven't made the kill in an hour, you'll rotate in. Same as always."

The others fanned out, leaving Bevel alone. This was Maddock's chance. He slithered forward like a cottonmouth in the mud, careful not to make a sound. He was grateful for the rush of the waterfall that helped to mask any sound he might make.

Bevel watched the men go, muttered a curse, and then sat down on a stone near the water's edge. He laid his rifle across his lap and fished into his shirt pocket for a cigarette and a lighter. Maddock tensed. At the instant the man's hands were occupied, his attention fully on lighting his smoke, Maddock pounced.

He covered the space between them in less than a second. By the time Bevel realized someone was there, Maddock had his gloved hand clamped firmly over the man's mouth, the keen blade of his knife at the man's throat.

"Make any loud sound or try to fight me, and I open your throat," he whispered. "Blink once if you understand." Bevel blinked one time, and rolled his wide eyes back, trying to catch a glimpse of Maddock. "I'm going to uncover your mouth so you can answer my questions. If you, move, cry out, or even talk too loud, I'll kill you. Blink once if you understand me." The man blinked, still trying to see who held him from behind, and Maddock removed his hand. "Are you hunting my friend?"

"N-no."

Maddock pressed the knife harder against the man's neck.

"Yes. Don't cut me. Please." Bevel's voice was a desperate whisper and his entire body trembled.

"Why are you doing this?"

"It's j-just what we do. All we got around here are deer, maybe a bear or a mountain lion sometimes. It ain't no challenge. People are more fun."

"You've done this before?" Maddock's stomach clenched and it was all he could do not to open the idiot's throat right then. "How many times?"

"A bunch. It's sort of a… tradition in these parts for generations. Nowadays the ranger is in charge. He lets Carter know when someone's going to be up here and he tells us. When we get the word, we drop everything and come quick."

"The police haven't investigated all these missing people?"

Bevel barked a short laugh. "They chalk it up to lost hikers, careless folk killed by animals, or bad falls."

"No one's ever gotten away to tell what the hell you're

doing up here?"

"Not a one. We always get 'em." The man smirked, unapologetic in the face of death.

Maddock's blood ran hot. "You've never hunted a SEAL before, have you?"

"A seal? We ain't got no seals around here. What do you think this is, California?"

"A Navy SEAL, you idiot. My friend was one, and so was I. You have no idea what you've gotten yourself into."

If Bevel had been pale before, his face went snow white at this new piece of information.

Maddock's thoughts raced. Should he just kill the man now? No. He would tie him up with his own shoelaces, gag him with his socks, and stow him in the back of the truck. Then he would take the rifle and go after Bones.

"I'm going to move around in front of you. When I do, I want you to very slowly get face-down on the ground. No noise, no sudden movements. You get me?"

"Yes."

Maddock released his grip on Bevel but kept his knife at the man's throat. He moved around in front of the man and instructed him to get down on the ground. Bevel complied, sinking to his knees. And that was when he made a fatal mistake.

Bevel lurched to one side, rolling over and coming up with a .22 caliber pistol. Maddock was on him before he could pull the trigger, pinning his gun hand to the ground and burying his knife in Bevel's heart. Just to be safe, he covered Bevel's mouth and nose, and watched him expire. When he was sure the man was dead, Maddock relieved him of his pistol and his ammunition belt, which held spare bullets both for the hunting rifle and the pistol.

He dragged Bevel's body into the reeds and hastily covered it over with mud and debris. When the next man came to take his turn at guard duty, hopefully that person would think Bevel had grown impatient and joined the hunt early, and not grow suspicious. Maddock and Bones were going to need every advantage they could get.

His pulse pounding, he slipped on the ammunition belt, tucked the pistol inside his suit, hefted the rifle, and set out on a little hunting expedition of his own.

When you're waiting *in a doctor's office, five minutes is an eternity. When you're being hunted, it flies by.*

Strangely, Bones was not frightened. Perhaps it was due to the surreal nature of the situation in which he found himself. Of course, this was far from the first time his life had been in danger, and he'd always come out alive. Deep inside, he always assumed things would somehow turn out all right.

Now he kept his eyes peeled as he dashed through the woods, looking for something that could give him an advantage. He stopped to pick up several fist-sized stones and stuff them into his pockets. He kept moving, and soon he was running along the base of a twenty-foot rock wall. This could be it. He hastily spied out cracks and outcroppings that would serve as handholds, and clambered up. It wasn't an easy climb, but rock walls were one of his specialties and, in short order, he was at the top and hidden in a thicket of hemlock. He waited, all his senses alive and attuned to every sound, every motion in the forest.

He was rewarded in a matter of minutes. A bearded man in a John Deere cap came trotting along the base of the cliff. It was one of those who arrived last. Bones did not know his name and didn't care. As the man passed below him, Bones raised up and threw one of the stones he had picked up as hard as he could.

The missile struck the man on the crown of his head, crumpling him to the ground. After looking around for other hunters and seeing none, Bones climbed back down to where the man lay. He rolled the fellow over onto his back and removed his cap to reveal a split scalp and a fractured skull. The wound was probably fatal, but Bones couldn't take the chance that he would survive. After all, this guy had been hunting him like an animal and would have shot him for the sheer pleasure of it if he'd gotten the chance.

Bones growled at the memory of the men taunting him, laughing as they sent him running into the woods. He dragged the dying man off the trail and finished him off by strangling him with his own belt. It should have been grisly work to Bones, but these were no longer human beings to him. They were targets to be eliminated.

One down.

The man up ahead of Maddock was making too much noise, carelessly crushing dry leaves and twigs underfoot. Either he was a complete idiot or he didn't suspect danger was anywhere nearby. Probably a bit of both.

With so many threats out there, Maddock needed to dispatch the hunter in front of him as quietly as possible.

He didn't want to use the rifle unless there was no alternative. Even if the other hunters heard the shot and believed it was one of their own shooting at Bones, it would still draw them toward the sound and they would be wary.

Careful to remain silent, he slid the rifle beneath a thick mountain laurel and placed the ammunition belt atop it. He tucked the dive bag holding the tomahawk inside his suit, drew his knife and pistol, and silently crept up on the unsuspecting hunter. Much more cautious than the lummox he stalked, he moved with catlike grace, choosing his footfalls with care. He was keenly aware of the danger he was in as he closed the distance between them. There was no cover along the last intervening twenty paces. If the man heard or sensed his approach, well, Maddock would probably get him first with the .22, but unless he managed a head shot, the fellow just might put a round or two into Maddock with his Remington. A voice inside Maddock's head pointed out that he had never fired this particular pistol, so he had no idea of its accuracy or firing tendencies. He shut the voice up, since the point was now moot.

Fifteen feet...

Ten feet...

Five feet...

The man finally realized someone was coming and whirled around. He was too late to bring his rifle to bear, but the barrel smashed into Maddock's left hand, knocking the .22 free. Maddock lashed out with the knife, catching the man across the throat, but it was a shallow slice, barely worse than a cut from shaving. His opponent instinctively drew back, but before Maddock could stab him in the gut, the man struck Maddock with the butt of his rifle. Maddock took the blow on the back of his left shoulder, turning with it. He spun, brought the knife around in a wide arc, and drove it backhanded into the man's neck just above his right shoulder. The man roared in pain and panic.

He fired his rifle, but the shot went wild. Maddock yanked his knife free and silenced him with a hard left to the temple that sent him crumpling to the ground. He would have died quickly from the neck wound, but Maddock didn't want the others to hear any sound from the dying man.

Too late.

Feet crashed through the undergrowth. Something buzzed past his head and clipped a bough from the pine tree behind him. At least one of the others had been much closer than he expected! He took off back the way he had come, weaving between any bits of cover he could find.

"He got Jason!" The cry was punctuated with another shot that barely missed. He dodged to his right into a dense stand of pines. Limbs smacked his face and pine cones pierced his bare feet as he ran. In the stillness of the forest he could hear the men's voices as plain as day.

"How'd he get behind us, Pa?"

"He's an Indian. I suppose they have tricks. We'll have to be careful."

"Bevel will get him if he heads back to the clearing. I'm going after him!"

Maddock spotted a low-growing patch of rhododendron and dove beneath it. He wormed his way in as far as he could go and waited. The footsteps came closer and two sets of booted feet trotted past his hiding place. They would figure out soon enough that Bevel wouldn't be getting anyone ever again. He gave them time to get out of earshot and then headed back toward the place where he'd hidden the rifle. He had not made it far when he heard more voices.

"He's dead," said a calm, confident voice.

"Who do you think done it, Carter? Was it the Indian?"

"Unless you think someone else is out here. But why wouldn't he take Jason's rifle? It's strange. And whose pistol is this?"

Maddock crept silently away. Now he had two men on either side of him, and only his knife for a weapon. On a positive note, he could now account for six of the seven men, two of them were permanently accounted for, and it appeared that none of them had yet gotten Bones.

He moved into deeper cover among the trees that lined the sloping valley wall. When he was far enough away to feel safe stopping for a few moments, he took time to rub dirt on his face, and did his best to dirty his dive suit with more of the rich, black earth before moving on. He soon came to a spot where time and weather had eroded a deep, winding channel up the side of the mountain. It would likely provide an easy passage to the top, but he hesitated, fearing he might stumble upon the seventh hunter around a blind turn. Instead, he chose a more difficult way up the slope, keeping in sight of the channel, but behind cover as much as he could.

The sound of the waterfall grew louder as he climbed and he emerged on a ledge overlooking the lake and valley below. The two men who had shot at him were standing alongside the vehicles. The older of the two was speaking animatedly, emphasizing his points by poking the younger man in the chest. If either were to look this way, they would spot Maddock in an instant. That gave him an idea. But how best to put it into effect?

Limbs slapped Bones in the face as he dashed through the forest. Breaking into a clearing, he had to watch his step as the holes of long-ago rotted stumps made his path a veritable mine field. He leaped across a deep gap where the game trail he followed had eroded into one of the holes and landed on an uneven patch of ground. His ankle rolled and hot pain coursed through his leg.

He had caught a glimpse of two men who were pursuing him. He had a good lead on them, but they definitely had his trail. He'd tried to hide signs of his passing as much as he could, but it had not thrown them off. He caught a glimpse of sunlight and blue sky up ahead. The forest was thinning out. Perhaps there was an end to this valley, maybe even a road, or some other sign of civilization.

He burst through the undergrowth and came skidding to a halt. The tips of his booted feet slid over the edge of a sheer cliff. The drop was hundreds of feet to the rocks below. No wonder his pursuers had no fear of him escaping. The wooded area through which he ran had neatly funneled him to this dead end. Could he double back and work his way past them or at least get back to high ground? They would expect him to end up here, so they would be moving this way. How could he use that to his advantage? A thought struck him and he hurried back to the clearing.

He had done this many times before, so the task was a simple one, and in less than a minute he had dug the hole in the trail even deeper and covered it over with twigs, leaves, and earth. Ideally, he'd have dug a pit and placed sharpened stakes at the bottom, but he lacked the time or tools to create such a trap. When the Viet Cong had made traps like this one, they smeared the sharpened stakes with their own feces in order to give the victim a septic infection. He grinned at the thought of one of these inbreeders impaled on a sharpened crapstick. Too bad he couldn't go that route. In this case, he just needed to distract his pursuers long enough for him to get away.

He melted into the brush near the cliff and began working his way back in the direction of the battlefield. In a matter of seconds he heard the stealthy approach of his stalkers. He froze, knowing that any movement could give him away. He watched as the men, the younger in the lead, followed by Carter, the big, paunchy guy who seemed to be the leader of the group, moved along the path. They were quiet, for white guys, and moved well in the woods; he'd give them that much. Thirty yards from where he watched, the young man stepped right into Bones' trap, gave a yelp of surprise, and fell face-first onto the trail.

Bones fired off two quick shots at Carter, but the man had reacted the moment the ground gave way beneath his companion's feet. Moving faster than Bones would have believed possible for a man of his bulk and girth, he dived to the ground and rolled behind a tree. Bones' shots sizzled through empty air. He flattened out behind a stump, cursing his luck.

Now up on all fours, the younger man scrambled for his rifle. Bones squeezed off a carefully-aimed shot that took his target in the head. Carter cried out in fear and rage at the sight. Bones snapped off another shot in the direction of the cry and then ran as fast as his injured ankle would permit.

Bullets shredded the greenery around him. He dodged to his right, trying to put an oak tree between himself and his attacker, but just before he moved behind the tree, fire lanced across his chest, and he heard the rifle's report. He had been shot.

There wasn't time to do more than glance at the bloody streak across his pectoral muscles, but he could tell it was not a serious wound. He paused behind the tree long enough to fire off another shot in the direction of his attacker before taking off again. He wondered if the gunfire would draw the other hunters. He assumed it would, but at least he had taken care of another of them. Somehow, he had to find Maddock and get the hell out of here.

Maddock pressed his body into the hollow of an old oak tree, gripping the strange tomahawk he had found in the cave. Shielded on his other side by a fir, he would be nigh-invisible to anyone headed up the wash, and he had reason to believe someone would be coming soon. He had prepared his trap and then let himself be spied crossing the top of the ridge. He had been certain to look like he was on the move, in hopes the men would not expect an ambush. Now he waited.

Soon, he heard the faint scuff of a booted foot on stone. Whoever was climbing the wash was being careless. Maddock prayed the man was equally unobservant. His prayer was answered moments later with a loud thwack and a shout of surprise and pain and the sound of something metal clattering to the ground. Maddock sprang from his hiding place and leapt into the wash, the tomahawk upraised, but when his eyes fell on the man, he saw there was no need for the weapon.

It was Nathan, the youngest of the hunters. His eyes were wide in death and his mouth hung open. His first blood had been his own.

Maddock had found a springy sapling growing chest-high out of a crack in the stone just before a sharp bend in the rock, tied his dive knife to it, bent it back and fixed it in place, then set a trip line made of vine. It was one of the many tricks he'd picked up during his time as a SEAL. He had expected it to distract and hopefully injure his enemy, but he was gratified to see that the knife had found the young man's heart. Perhaps he should feel bad about taking the life of a youth of no more than twenty, but he could muster no sympathy for one who would hunt another man like an animal. He took the dead man's rifle and recovered his knife, which he wiped on the man's shirt. Another one down.

If only he could find Bones, they could get out of this mess. Of course, he had heard shouts and gunfire somewhere down below. He hoped that meant Bones was taking care of business. Bones had to be all right.

He spotted a flash of movement in the undergrowth below. It was barely more than a momentary glimpse. He froze, looking and listening, but he neither saw nor heard anything else. He knew only one person who could move like that.

"Bones?" In the quiet, his whisper sounded louder than any gunshot.

"Maddock?" Bones melted out of the nearby trees. Blood soaked his shirt, but he otherwise looked strong.

"About time you showed up. How many did you get?"

"Three."

"You suck. I've only gotten two. The next one is mine, and we can flip for the last." He looked around, finally catching sight of Nathan's body. "Nice booby trap, Maddock. I guess you used your knife?" Maddock nodded. "Good. I didn't like that kid. Didn't have proper respect for his elders."

Each filled the other in on the events that had brought them to this point. Bones cursed when Maddock told him what he had learned from Bevel about the corrupt park ranger and the self-styled hunters of men.

Suddenly, a bestial cry of pain and rage shattered the silence. Maddock immediately dropped to his belly and pointed his rifle in the direction of the cry. From his hiding place, he could see that Nathan's father had found his son's body. Maddock inched forward, looking for a clear shot. Bones wormed up alongside him.

"My turn," Bones whispered.

But there was no need for either of them to take the shot. Letting loose an anguished wail, Nathan's father let his rifle fall to the ground, drew a pistol from his belt, and put it in his mouth. Maddock closed his eyes as the sound of the shot echoed through the canyon.

"Wimp." Bones face split in a wicked grin. "It's not like it's the first death you've ever seen."

"I don't know, man." Maddock grimaced. "Suicide just seems like it should be a... private thing." Nathan's father deserved no sympathy. In fact, Maddock would have killed him without remorse, yet he took no pleasure from watching a death. Sometimes, killing needed to be done, but there was always a part of him that found it regrettable.

"We can talk philosophy later. Did you find it?"

It took Maddock a moment to realize Bones was asking about the tomahawk. "Oh, sorry dude. All I found was one of those rubber-tipped spears like you guys sell to little kids. Oh, and an Indian taco."

Bones's eyes, which had fallen at the word "sorry," widened as he realized Maddock was messing with him. "Hand it over, bro. Now!"

Maddock drew the stone tomahawk from his bag and held it out.

Bones gasped. He took the tomahawk in trembling hands and held it up. His eyes glowed, and his grin was almost beatific as he gazed on his ancestor's treasure.

"This is really it," he whispered. "I didn't dare believe it was possible, but this is really it."

"So what is it?" Maddock thought it was a fine example of craftsmanship, but apparently there was much more to the artifact.

"Tenskwatawa." His voice was solemn and reverent. "The brother of Tecumseh. This was his tomahawk." He lowered his hands and his eyes met Maddock's. "Thanks, bro. You don't know what this means to me."

"I've never heard of him. Who was he?"

"They called him The Prophet. It's too long a story to tell you right now, but this thing has power." He admired it for a moment longer before tucking it into his belt and rising to his feet. "I'll tell you more later. Let's find our friend Carter and show him what it's like to be hunted."

They made their way to the cliff that overlooked the battlefield, lake, and vehicles. "We're almost too late." Maddock pointed to the spot where a figure had just broken from the cover of the forest and was lumbering toward the parked trucks and jeeps. Carter.

Bones smiled and raised his rifle.

"That's a long shot." Maddock arched an eyebrow. "Think you can make it?"

Bones only grinned more broadly as he gently squeezed the trigger. Far below them, Carter fell flat on his face. "Dinner's on you for doubting me."

"You can even think about eating after all this?" Maddock rubbed his temples. "I hate to say this, but even though we're in the right, I don't know what chance we'd have of getting any kind of justice around here. Hell, in a town like this, the judge, jury, and victims are probably all first cousins. I think we need to dispose of the bodies, pitch the rifles into the lake, and get the hell out of Dodge."

"You're right." Bones drew the tomahawk from where he had tucked it into his belt. "But if what they say about this tomahawk is true, we won't have any trouble dealing with the bodies. After that, I've got one more loose end I'm going to tie up."

Words failed Maddock as they drove away from the battlefield. In the end, they had wiped and disposed of all the rifles and pistols, save Carter's antique Colt which Bones had insisted on keeping as a souvenir, though Maddock thought he was crazy. By the time Bones had used the tomahawk to... dispose of the bodies, though, he was certain the names of the seven dead men would simply be added to the list of strange disappearances in Dark Entry. Maddock had seen and experienced some strange things in the time he and Bones had known one another, but what Bones had done with that tomahawk was near the top of the list. The bears emerging silently from the trees and dragging away the bodies. The coyotes lapping up… He shuddered at the memory. He supposed he would never grow accustomed to the idea that there were forces in this world that defied understanding.

When they were a quarter of a mile from the ranger station, he pulled the car off the shoulder of the road and cut the engine.

Bones grabbed his arm before he could open the door and get out. "You sure you want to be a part of this? I can take care of it myself."

"They were hunting both of us." Maddock felt the heat rising inside of him as he thought about what the men had tried to do to them. The way he saw it, justice had been meted out, but there was one more person who needed to pay. There was no telling how many murders could be laid at the man's feet.

"I know." Bones looked up at the night sky. "It's just that you and I are different, Maddock. You're… better than me. You've always killed in combat, or self-defense."

"And you haven't?"

"Well, still. I don't want you to…"

"Don't worry about it. My conscience is clear on this one. Besides, we're not going to do anything to the man. At least, not if your plan works."

Bones gingerly drew his backpack from the back seat and held it at arm's length. He clutched the tomahawk in his other hand. He and Maddock had washed up in the lake and changed into clean clothes, but Maddock thought he could almost see a specter of something sinister in his friend's face.

"It will work. It worked back at Dark Entry, didn't it?"

Maddock grimaced at the memory and nodded. It certainly had worked and he would never forget it. "Let's get on with it then."

Earl Eddings checked his watch for what must have been the twentieth time. He should have heard from Carter by now. He wanted to call and make sure everything was all right, but that was strictly forbidden. Their connection had to be carefully hidden. Carter had already let too many people in on their little game. Perhaps it was time to put an end to it. He'd made a nice chunk of change out of the deal, Carter and his friends had their fun, and together they'd made sure the deaths were always written off as missing persons or tragic accidents. Perhaps they were tempting fate by keeping things going. Of course, getting out of the arrangement would be neither simple nor easy.

He propped his feet up on the desk and reached for his coffee. It had gone cold, but he didn't feel like brewing another pot. Besides, once he heard from Carter, he'd close the office and retire to his apartment in the back. He'd heat up a frozen pizza, watch a movie, maybe Smokey and the Bandit, and hit the sack. He swished the bitter drink around in his mouth and closed his eyes, trying to coax a bit of flavor from it. Paul Revere and the Raiders were on the radio. It was a good song, one of his favorites.

"I hope I'm not interrupting anything."

Eddings' eyes snapped open as the coffee cup fell from his limp fingers. It was the Indian from earlier today. How could he be here? He got a grip on himself and forced a smile.

"Not at all, you just gave me a start, that's all." He sat up, letting his feet fall to the floor. "Did you find the battlefield all right?" The Indian didn't appear to have a gun, just a backpack. Still smiling, Eddings let his hand drift toward the bottom drawer of his desk where he kept his .38 revolver.

"Keep your hands where we can see them." Another man had slipped through the door while Eddings' eyes were on the Indian. He was shorter than the Indian, not quite six feet, with close-cropped blond hair, blue-gray eyes, and a calm demeanor that was somehow even more intimidating than the seething rage that boiled behind the Indian's eyes. He held a pistol trained on Eddings, and it was readily apparent that the man had both the ability and inclination to use it if he so desired.

Eddings recognized the gun. "So your plan is to kill me with Carter's gun and hope it gets pinned on him?" He forced a laugh. "You two don't understand. This is bigger than me. You kill me, you're just sticking your hand into the viper's nest."

"Funny you should mention snakes." The Indian deftly unzipped his backpack and upended it, spilling two twisting, black-banded forms onto the desk. Timber rattlers! They were each a good four feet long, and they both immediately coiled as if to strike, rattles buzzing, and eyes locked on Eddings.

"What is this?" Eddings tried to keep his voice calm, but it came out as a hoarse whisper. Do you think you can make these things do your bidding?" The thought was absurd but, seeing the way these snakes kept their eyes trained on him, he believed, against all rational thought, the Indian could do exactly that.

"Oh, you wouldn't believe what I can do." The Indian pulled a black stone tomahawk from his belt and slowly drew the blade across his palm. He squeezed his fist and let the blood drip down onto the tomahawk, which seemed to sparkle as if shooting stars whirled inside it. The Indian's eyes remained locked on Eddings as he raised the tomahawk to his lips and whispered a single word.

The snakes struck as one. Eddings screamed as the fangs bit into him again and again, hot pain searing his body, burning through the numbing disbelief that clouded his senses. The agony seemed to go on forever. And then it stopped.

He watched through cloudy eyes as the rattlesnakes slithered off his desk, dropped to the floor, and disappeared. As light and life fled, he saw the Indian make a mocking bow, turn, and walk away.

The End

VENOM

‘

Coauthored with Matt James

When National Geographic reporter Makenzie Moore needs a guide to take her into the depths of the Amazon, she calls on former Navy SEAL turned treasure hunter Bones Bonebrake. Following a string of disappearances and strange sightings, they hope to discover a new species of super predator. Eyewitnesses agree on one detail about the creature that lurks in the jungle—it's really, really big.

This is where things get weird. A few years ago, Matt James and I published this novella as part of a special Kindle program. That program closed shortly after this book was published.

As I went through the process of revising and republishing each of the books from that program, I realized that if I had it to do over, I would tell the story in a very different way. I retold that story in *Serpent- A Dane Maddock Adventure.*

Next, I tried to move the plot of *Venom* to a different continent and give it a different monster. While I was able to follow the general plot structure and save a few bits and pieces of prose, that book, *Lost City*, also ended up being a very different book.

Since *Venom* was shelved, I have received many emails from readers who missed it on its initial publication. Join Bones for another trip into the Peruvian

Amazon in search of Yacumama. I hope you enjoy this different take on the legend.

1

Feet propped up on the railing, he relaxed as the POS riverboat chugged along. With each bob of the small craft, the rickety handrail beneath his boots felt like it was about to give out at any moment. But it had taken him a while to get semi-comfortable, and he wasn't about to change his incline for something as inconsequential as the destruction of someone else's property.

As a former Navy SEAL, Uriah "Bones" Bonebrake, loved the water. What he didn't like was limping along the Amazon River without so much as a paddle...or an ice-cold beer to wet his whistle. All he had on board was lukewarm bottled water and whatever else he brought along with him.

Why was Bones back in the Amazon? Well, he got a call from someone he knew—someone he'd only just met, actually. Nico Russo, a new acquaintance from Cabras, Sardinia, had called Bones, telling him that some chick had come asking about the events that had taken place there. That lady had an offer too good for Nico not to tell Bones. Nico wanted to help also, but couldn't. He was stuck still playing the role of watchdog in his hometown.

Where did a journalist get that kind of bread? Bones thought, scratching his chin. He mentally replayed his adventure in the small island town of Cabras last month. Like most of his exploits, that one was a doozy.

Bones and his partner, Dane Maddock, were at the forefront of that area of expertise, adventure, albeit, out of the public limelight. Maddock didn't like to boast about their proficiency at finding rare and valuable antiquities, but Bones loved too. They were awesome at finding the stuff, and they had made a damned good living doing so for...

How many years now?

Bones couldn't believe how long they had been at it since they both left the navy. Most of the time, they worked together, solving ridiculous riddles while battling unbelievable enemies. It was something straight out of a comic book or even a campy action-adventure novel.

Anyway, the chick that had contacted Bones... She was a real firecracker from what Nico said, a tall red-head that worked for the renowned National Geographic. Her name was Mackenzie Moore, and she had apparently gone to Cabras to investigate the happenings surrounding Bones' involvement there.

Bones still couldn't fully believe what he had seen. Giants from ancient times were alive and well beneath the surface of Sardinia. At least, they were alive and well. Bones had a hand in wiping out their monstrous king. Whether the species was genuinely extinct or not was something Nico was still looking into. Hence him staying behind and not joining Bones in Brazil.

Bones had been at his favorite local spot in Key West, sipping on his third Dos Equis when the bartender called him over, saying he had a call. Bones' only reaction was to lift a single eyebrow at the man who returned his questioned look with a soft nod. Standing tall, Bones stretched his six-foot-six frame, cracked his neck, and made for the bartop. Then, he was handed the phone, and before he could ask who was on the other end, she got right to the chase.

"Mr. Bonebrake, my name is Mackenzie Moore, and

I have a job for you." Her voice was bold and hard. Nico's description of the caller was on point so far. He recalled Nico describing her furious response after finding out nothing about giants in Cabras.

This should be fun. He sighed. She'll probably welcome me with open arms.

Bones shook his head, clearing the memory away, focusing on the setting sun. From its height, Bones figured they were due to arrive at their destination soon. Mackenzie, or "Mack" as she preferred, was seeing to their supplies in a village up ahead somewhere. She had arrived a few days prior and wanted to get a jump on things.

"At least she's punctual," he said to himself, picturing the columnist. Mack was tall and tended to wear her red hair in a ponytail. Bones understood the reason, having long hair himself—especially in a place as humid as the Amazon. Like her, Bones also preferred to wear his shoulder-length, black hair up, relieving himself of the unyielding heat and mucky wetness the region regularly assaulted you with.

"Mr. Bone," a voice said, announcing the boat captain's presence, a man who could barely understand English. Instead of calling him Bones, the short local repeatedly called him "Bone." If it were someone else getting called Bone, Bones would've been laughing his Injun ass off. But it wasn't someone else...and Bones was annoyed as hell.

While somewhat fluent in Spanish, Bones was iffy with Portuguese, the national language of Brazil. Some words resembled those he knew in Spanish—some didn't. The cozy village of Encantador was just around the next bend, and it was to be his meeting place with Mack.

Encantador, he thought, translating the word.

Lovely, or enchanting… Somehow, even without actually seeing the place, Bones knew it would be something else entirely. He had been to plenty of Podunk-like places in his life, this would be no exception.

"Please have working commodes."

He really didn't want to have to "drop off the kids" in a hole in the ground. Knowing his luck, he'd probably squat down next to a poisonous plant. It would bring an all new meaning to the term redskin.

Bones loved to make people uncomfortable with his humor—what he thought was funny, anyway. It was an excellent way to test someone. While sometimes acting the part of the fool, Bones was as sharp as a knife…just a little rougher around the edges than most blades. He and Maddock both enjoyed a raunchy joke, but unlike Bones, Maddock wasn't one to repeat it aloud for all to hear.

Like the one about a priest, a rabbi, and an insurance salesman… Bones grinned at the punchline. What a whopper.

The "metropolis" that was Lovely, Brazil came into view, and to Bones' astonishment, it wasn't entirely a crap heap. In reality, it was actually a decent looking place from where he stood. Even from where he was, Bones could see what looked like a tall wall built into the tree line behind the "city" limits, a couple hundred feet away at most. He shook his head. Here he was, in the middle of the Amazon, and he was approaching the closest thing to a Jurassic Park gate as he had ever seen.

"Just freaking wonderful…"

They chugged closer and, as they neared, Bones turned his attention to a tall, lean figure stepping out of what passed for a dockside lounge. She, and it was definitely a "she" based on her feminine figure, crossed her arms, looking very impatient.

Am I late?

He looked down at his watch, still wearing the hi-tech Apple device that Tam gave him and Maddock in Norway.

Nope, right on time.

Tamara Broderick was a CIA spook that ran an arm of the "Company" called the Myrmidon Squad. She would occasionally reach out to Bones and Maddock if she needed something within their professional wheelhouse found. Off-the-books stuff. Very hush-hush. The watch itself was linked to a satellite that didn't technically exist and would never lose connection unless he went deep underground.

Please, no more caves. Bones had seen plenty of those recently.

Bones' current job in Brazil wasn't one of those Tam-involved missions, though. This was just a look-and-find, paid for by an employee of National Geographic with the knowledge that Bones' identity wouldn't be used in the story. The stipulation was a caveat that Bones never operated without. It was his preferred way to work, especially with all the people looking for him and his team back home in the Keys.

He usually would've used an alias, but Mack had already known his real identity. So that was off the table.

At first, Bones was skeptical of the job as a whole. What she offered him was a ton of money for a globe-hopping journalist to dish out, especially with no "hard" evidence to speak of.

Earlier in the week, Mack had sent over everything she had on the subject in question. They were looking for a mythological creature that was well-known in the region but not so much anywhere else. Yacumama, the "water mother," was a sea monster entrenched within a large population of South American tribes. It was said to be a monstrous fifty paces long. If Bones' math was correct, fifty paces equaled roughly 125 feet.

He softly whistled at the number, still stunned.

While most believed the Yacumama was some kind of overexaggerated anaconda or even a living relative to the extinct Titanoboa, Bones knew better than to jump to conclusions. Yes, the stories made it out to be just a gigantic species of snake, but still… The only other cryptid on Bones' list that both resembled a snake and was said to live within the Amazonian jungle was the Minhocao.

The Minhocao supposedly belonged to the caecilian group of animals. It was, in essence, a humungous earthworm, but was most likely just another tall tale revolving around a larger-than-life, limbless amphibian. The Maya depicted it in their art but obviously had no idea what they were looking at. They had no reference to compare to the creature. So, they called it as they saw it.

My kind of people.

Bones often acted with the same quick-thinking rationale. He had gotten himself into loads of trouble over the years by opening his large mouth—sometimes wide enough to park a semi in.

The boat docked minutes later, and Bones happily disembarked by merely grabbing his duffel bag and backpack and stepping over the loose, rotted-out railing. Pounding up the shaky anchorage, he got another good look at his employer.

Mack hadn't moved an inch to greet him. In fact, Bones wasn't sure she had even looked his way once since her eyes were hidden behind a pair of reflective aviator sunglasses. He stopped a few feet away and dropped his heavy duffel. Sticking out his hand, Bones went to formally introduce himself to the statue of a woman. Instead, Mack lashed out with a hard right and punched Bones in the jaw.

"That's for Cabras, asshole!" she shouted, ripping off her sunglasses and stepping into Bones' face. Bones had seen some pissed off chicks in his lifetime, but Mack put them all to shame.

2

Bones could only stand there, completely and utterly speechless. Then again, Mack never stopped screaming long enough for him to get a word in. She reiterated the fact that she had gone to Cabras a week after the incident with the Laestrygonians giants and the locals who served them.

What Bones didn't know was that Mack had almost lost her job in the process. She was currently suspended without pay and was using her savings to redeem herself. Bones knew no one in town would talk, so it didn't surprise him that Mack got nothing out of them.

Bones held up a single hand, quieting the still raging fireball. "First of all, don't do that crap again." He never once rubbed his chin. He wouldn't give her the satisfaction. "Secondly, when it comes to Cabras..." he looked her hard in the eyes, "steel vault. So, don't try." He looked away for a moment and opened his jaw wide, impressed at the strength of her punch.

He looked back at Mack, seeing a grin on her face.

"So," she said, "you were actually there?"

He sighed. Dammit, dude...

Picking up his duffle, he turned away from Mack and pounded down the rickety dock already done with this place. A few of the planks beneath him were so loose that they caused Bones to stumble, making his tough-guy gate feel awkward and embarrassing. In between steps, he heard Mack coming right up behind him.

Bones put on the brakes and stopped, satisfied when

she ran right into him. Bones was even more pleased when she let out an oof, followed by a bang and a splash. Glancing behind him, Bones smiled, seeing her sitting on her ass, glaring up at him. Her butt had broken through a piece of wood and hit water. Shaking his head, he smiled, faced her, and held out his hand. Bones could act like a jerk sometimes, but that didn't mean he was one.

"You done?" he asked.

Nostrils flared, Mack's anger eventually wilted, and her shoulders slumped. Next, she took Bones' offered hand, and he effortlessly hauled the lanky woman up. Bones made sure she was steady on her feet before letting go and heading off again.

"Hang on a second," he quickly added, holding out a strong arm, blocking Mack from continuing any further. "Is that why you brought me here, so you could punch me?"

Lifting a single finger, Mack shoved it into Bones' forearm which was draped across her chest like the arm of a guard gate. He let her go but didn't follow her right away. Stopping, she faced him and crossed her arms.

"If I did," she replied, "that would be one hell of an expensive punch."

Mack's right eyebrow raised slightly, getting a small smile out of Bones. While he liked the balls this chick had, he didn't like being lied to or conned.

Crossing his own arms, Bones waited.

She rolled her eyes. "Yes, part of me wanted you standing right here in front of me so I could knock your teeth in." She stepped up to him, stopping only a foot from him. "But no, I also need your expertise on things of this expedition's nature."

He grinned, raising an eyebrow, pleased that she had

just praised him. "And that is?"

She shook her head. "Geez, you really are full of yourself, aren't you?"

He shrugged. "More or less..." His eyes narrowed. "So, the Yacumama, huh?"

Mack stood straight, but instead of looking ready to talk, she looked...scared. Her eyes opened wide, and she did a quick look-see at who was listening in on their conversation. She even looked down the road...toward the medieval barrier.

A giant snake and King Kong-sized walls... He shoved his palm into his forehead and rubbed. Damn, damn, damn.

As it were, she and Bones were the only two people within earshot. The only other living thing near them was a pathetic looking dog. It looked up at him from its half-eaten fish and cocked its head to the side like all dogs did. Then, it huffed a sigh and returned its attention to its meal.

Mack motioned for him to sit on a crudely built bench near the water. Complying, Bones sat next to her and stayed silent, interested to know why she was acting so skittish.

"Yes, and no." She slid her sunglasses back on and continued. "Yes, we are here to confirm the existence of the Yacumama creature that's been said to have been seen recently."

"And the no?" Bones asked.

"Well," she replied, "this part of the jungle has its share of stories, and one of them is that a mythical serpent guards a horde of riches."

"So," he said, leaning back, "it's treasure then?"

"As well as the serpent, yes."

Bones scratched his head, unsure of why he was even thinking about it. He did this kind of thing all the time. So, he stood. "Shouldn't be a problem."

"Shouldn't?"

He shrugged. "Believe me when I say that anything can happen."

Especially with me involved.

He rubbed his forehead hard once more, still trying to figure out why he, in particular, was always getting into shenanigans like this. Well, not just him, anyways... Maddock and the rest of their team too. Bones was prepared to bring along a couple of his teammates but was instructed by Mack to come alone. It never bothered him before when he traveled by himself.

And it doesn't now.

He slipped back into his backpack. He wished he had his trusted Glock handgun tucked inside to make himself feel better. It always did. Bones didn't always need a pistol—he actually preferred to not need one. But if he was forced to use a gun, he was confident in doing so. He and Maddock were two of the best with firearms, continually debating one another that each was better than the other.

"We have a similar legend within the Cherokee, only ours is called the Tlanusi. Funny enough, it's supposed to be somewhere near where I'm from."

"And that is?" Mack asked, sounding genuinely interested.

He shook his head and moved the briefing along. "Doesn't matter. Tell me more about the eyewitness accounts."

Bones could tell that Mack wasn't used to not being in control. Typically, he'd feel somewhat sorry for someone in her position...maybe. But she hired him to lead them to victory, and victory could only be had if he knew everything there was to know.

"Fair enough," Mack said, pulling a classic pocket-sized pad of paper from the back of her jeans. She flipped through a few scribble-filled pages, eventually stopping on one. "Here it is, at least, here's one of them—the most recent."

"What about the other two sightings you mentioned on the phone?"

"We're getting there, big guy, hang on." She playfully patted Bones on the shoulder, all but confirming that she was finished being pissed at him. "This guy here…" she pointed to the page, "his name is Dr. Igor Fetisov, and he was once the most well-known herpetologist in Russia."

"Was?" he asked, forgoing the obvious joke that needed to be made. "What happened to him?"

"Igor disappeared over a year ago after he came here looking for a giant anaconda that had been spotted. It was said to be the largest ever in the region, and he wanted to study it." Mack flipped the page. "Well, he and a small team of locals went deeper into the rainforest and supposedly found something else."

"Our Yacumama?"

She nodded. "Or so says Igor. He got an excellent picture of it too, but to me, it just looks like the backend of your common anaconda. The lighting was a little dark, unfortunately." She looked behind them and then continued. "From what I've gathered, the one they found was most definitely the same snake Igor came here for, but instead of pursuing it like he had planned on doing, he changed courses and started asking questioning about the Yacumama legend."

"This doesn't make any sense," Bones said, retying

his hair. "A man like this doesn't go rogue for a myth. There has to be more."

Mack smiled and flipped the page.

"What?" he asked, stopping.

She faced him. "I wasn't done… Igor also said that there was something off about the water around them. Though it was hard to see with the dense canopy overhead, he said that, and I quote, 'when a small amount of sun hit the water, it shined like gold.'"

"Golden water," Bones said, chuckling softly, "you're kidding me?" Mack didn't laugh back. "Okay, Red," he kept going before she could object to the nickname, "explain to me how a mucky-ass river glowed gold in the middle of the Amazon rainforest?"

She smiled again.

"Dammit, stop grinning at me." He crossed his arms. "The only time a chick is allowed to look at me like that is after a couple of rounds on a Serta Perfect Sleeper."

Her face turned up. "Ugh… And, once again, I wasn't done."

Mack returned the small notepad into her back pocket and reached into her front left one. Keeping her hand tight around whatever she possessed, she stood and stepped uncomfortably close to Bones. Typically, he had no problem with a girl snuggling up close to him, but since he knew he had zero chance with Mack, he wanted to keep it professional between them.

"This is why I am here."

He looked down into her open hand. There, about the size of a half-dollar, was a brilliant gold coin. Engraved into its surface was a symbol he didn't recognize. It held two serpents, facing away from one another, and they were surrounded by a variation of what seemed to be

Mayan-inspired glyphs. It also looked hand carved and was slightly worn from the elements—in this case, probably water.

It made sense why Igor stayed in Brazil instead of returning home to Russia. A) Russian weather was the worst kind of awful. B) There was an untold fortune of gold somewhere out there.

He peered over Mack's head and took in the nearby tree line.

A lost tribe of Yacumama worshippers maybe?

It would explain the coin.

"Yes," she added, getting his attention, "there is more here than just our snake."

His eyes met hers. "Woah, mama."

Bones' mind started going over a number of different possibilities, delving deep into his long history of look-and-find missions like this. But another thing nagged at him too. Once more, he looked down at the coin in Mack's hand, seeing something he didn't like.

He tapped the center of the coin. "Why are there two snakes?"

3

Bones and Mack sat at the corner most table in the local dive-bar-hut. Facing what passed as the front door, a thin, wooden divider really, Bones wanted to be able to see if anyone was interested in their arrival. Before walking in, Mack explained that they would be fine.

"Places like Lovely thrive on tourism. It's far enough into the Amazon that it hasn't been picked clean, but close enough that it's not too remote."

Bones snorted out a laugh. "Ever hear of Vikersund, Norway? Or how about Cabras, Sardinia—before, well, you know…" Mack shook her head. "Exactly! Remote or not, trouble always comes calling when there is something to be gained. There are things going on in the world that you wouldn't believe."

"More unbelievable than a mythological, one-hundred-foot-long god-snake?" she countered.

"Absolutely." Bones was confident in his reply. "Most are just a ton weirder, though." He glanced at her. "Like, a lot weirder."

"Giants in Sardinia," she said matter-of-factly.

Bones shrugged, indifferent. "No idea what you're talking about."

Mack got defensive. "But you literally just said they were there!"

He raised an eyebrow. "Did I? No. I just mentioned the town, and you sprinted to the finish line all willy-nilly."

"Then why mention Cabras at all?"

He smiled. "Because, Red, annoying you makes me happier about being here."

"God, I hate you." Mack's hands came up to her face, and her elbows found the table. She rubbed hard and spoke, keeping her face covered, her voice muffled by her palms. "This is because I hit you, isn't it?"

Bones leaned back, satisfied. "Yup." He leaned in. "Plus, did it ever occur to you that it might not be my decision to keep whatever happened in Cabras a secret? Do I look like I work for any kind of government agency?" He flexed his arms, chest, and shoulder muscles beneath his tight, black shirt, and grinned. "I'm never one to turn down fortune and glory."

Before Mack could respond, a little, horribly wrinkled, old woman came over to them and asked if they'd like to order something. Bones glanced to his left, surprised that he was looking eye to eye with the very short local. She couldn't have even been five-feet-tall. If he stood, Bones would've towered over her like he did most children.

"Food?"

Bones silently waved a hand, answering her in the negative. If he got hungry, he'd snack on something from inside his bag. Like a lot of third-world countries, or in this case, third-world villages, Bones avoided any and all food from them. Montezuma's Revenge was nothing to joke about—even though he loved himself a good poop joke.

"Food, yes?"

Bones just turned his body toward her and gave her the meanest looking scowl he could muster. Even it didn't work... The old lady just stood there nodding empathically. She wasn't going to take no for an answer.

Either that, or she didn't actually understand the simple body language and hand gestures. He knew one gesture that would no doubt tell the old bag to get lost, but he couldn't get himself to give the wrinkled bird the finger.

He groaned, and before he could tell her off one more time, someone else stepped up next to her. He spoke in whatever passed as Lovely's local dialect. It wasn't pure Portuguese either. It was a hybrid of it and something else.

The woman nodded again, showing them a mouthful of missing teeth as they both looked Bones and Mack's way. Then, she disappeared behind another group of locals, vanishing like a ghost. The man, someone half her age, stepped up and took her place. He was also a native, but was barely taller than the—

"That your mother?" Bones asked, seeing the vertically-challenged family resemblance.

"Yes," he said looking like he wanted to say something nasty to Bones.

"Wonderful woman," Mack slid in, deflating whatever angst Bones had caused. Bones' eyes found hers, and he nonverbally thanked her with a soft nod.

'Shorty' smiled, also missing most of his teeth.

Another family trait...

He turned to Mack. "Ms. Moore?"

Mack's eyes flicked quickly to Bones, looking very worried that the guy recognized her. Bones balled his fist beneath the table ready to lash out at him at a moment's notice. The time never came, however.

"I am Dudu, your contact, and guide."

"Hang on, man!" Bones couldn't hold back a laugh. "Your name is Dudu?" Bones snickered loudly again. "Seriously, bro, did Caca call in sick or something?"

Dudu didn't join in, nor did he seem to understand

the jab. Bones waited an eternity before giving up on anyone having a chuckle with him. He knew it was immature, but how could you not laugh at someone named Dudu?

Mack politely held out her hand. "Hello, um, Dudu, yes, my name is Mackenzie Moore. This," she tipped her chin at Bones, "is Bones?"

Dudu grinned. "Bones?" His eyebrows scrunched, lost in deep thought. "Such an unusual name."

Bones' mouth hung open, unable to formulate a proper response. The corner of Mack's mouth twitched. She was clearly holding back a smile, thinking the turnaround on Bones was hilarious.

Dudu thought that Bones' name was the odd one at the table? It wasn't the first time Bones had gotten a sideways glance from someone, questioning his name. This, however, took the cake.

Dudu continued. "When would you like to leave?"

"Where's Dr. Fetisov?" Mack asked. "He's supposed to be joining us. We need his knowledge of snakes."

The local man bit his lip.

"What happened?" Bones asked, knowing that look.

"It is Igor…" Dudu replied quietly, leaning in closer to them, "he has gone missing."

"Explain." Bones wasn't messing around. While no longer a SEAL, he still carried some of the natural traits—instincts—of one. If someone went missing, someone they needed to get their job done especially, then he wanted to know everything he could and help any way he could.

"Igor went back to the river to search for more…you know…" Dudu looked over his shoulder, nervous to talk about the gold that was found, "and he and the two men he took never came back. That was five days ago."

His English is really good. But Bones didn't much care how, or why, the man spoke it so well. It would help, that was for sure. His fluency in the language didn't matter as much as the whereabouts of their missing scientist was all.

"The coin?" Bones asked quietly, looking at Mack.

"Left for me," she replied, thinking. "Maybe he left it behind because he knew someone could come looking for it?

"Could be…" Bones said, thinking hard.

"But who?" Mack asked. "I thought he left it because was going to be gone a day or two max." Her shoulders slumped. "Not go missing for good."

Dudu opened his mouth, but instead of adding to the powwow, a scream and a crash rang out around them. The commotion was coming from just outside the small "restaurant," and Bones immediately bolted for the door to check it out. Swinging open the feeble, wooden door, Bones almost ripped it from its' hinges when he saw what was on the other side.

Three men were marching down the main road, heading toward the dock. Bones and Mack had been inside the first building past them, the one he saw her exit upon arriving in Lovely. He knew it wasn't a coincidence or bad luck either. Whoever these guys were, they were here for them.

For the coin.

"Stay put," he called back, unsure of what to make of the newcomers.

"Like hell I am," Mack replied.

He spun on her, and with a clenched jaw, he said, "Stay. Put."

Gritting her own teeth, Mack gave him a look that

said she wasn't happy, but it was also one of understanding. Bones was trying to protect her, and while he knew she could handle herself reasonably well, few could go toe-to-toe with Bones on his best day.

Even if it was three on one.

"Oh, crap..."

Just then, the three men turned on him in unison, like they were being controlled by a third party with a joystick. Each man's head cocked to the side, and they squinted. It was as strange of behavior as he'd ever seen—and that was saying something. He had seen a lot, for sure.

"Come on, dudes, let's talk about this for a sec—" he paused any attempt at defusing the situation when he saw their eyes...their gold eyes. Their pupils were still black, but their irises were a solid gold color. Even the whites of their eyes were a gross milky-gold color.

"Knocking back the local shine a little hard, don't you think?"

Neither one of them reacted.

"Seriously, you guys need to see a doctor before that crap spreads."

And it had.

As one, like they had just received orders via a mental link, the three "infected" locals removed their shirts, exposing their upper bodies to those gathered around them. Each man had identical golden scales running up their chests, as well as across their shoulders. From where Bones was standing, he couldn't tell if it also covered their backs, but he figured he'd get a good look any moment. The only differences in them were that one of the men had more of the growths.

Infected for longer?

Women and children shrieked in horror, as did

some of the weak-stomached men. They all fled, rambling to one another like they had seen this before. Seen this before…

What the hell is going on with this place?

The only one that didn't take a step back in fright was Bones. He, like in most cases, stepped toward this conflict. He never backed down.

Ever.

4

Wanting nothing more than to end the debate quickly and just draw his pistol and shoot the trio of jackasses, Bones cursed himself for not having one. Instead, he balled his fists but refrained from raising them. He wanted these guys to make the first move.

When they did, they attacked as one, perfectly synchronizing their efforts. But it wasn't the choreography that caught Bones' attention the most. It was the way they did it, hacking and slashing at him with their fingernails while hissing like, well, snakes. The pricks even had pointed teeth resembling those of a serpent's.

One went high, and another went low. Bones kicked at the one going for his knees, backhanding the other's hand away from his face. The third was… Bones couldn't find him.

What the—

He growled as something cut through the back of his shirt, digging into the meat of his left shoulder blade. Spinning, Bones caught the unseen assailant in the side of the head with a hard elbow, knocking him to the ground with the single blow. The quick knockout gave him some confidence that he could dispatch the two remaining men with equally brutal efficiency.

It also helps that they're small, he thought, keeping still as the two remaining men circled him like vultures.

Thankfully, Bones' attackers were, on average, a foot shorter than him. His longer reach and more powerful build meant he should be able to end this fight soon rather than later. A searing pain across his back crippling him to the point that he folded in on himself, causing him to cry out in agony.

"Argh!" he shouted, swinging wildly at anything that moved. He squeezed his eyes shut and waited for the torture to subside. Unfortunately, it didn't. What wasn't unfortunate was that Bones wasn't alone in this fight.

A high-pitched scream announced the arrival of Mack. Bones figured she'd join the fray eventually. He barely knew her, but what he did know is that she was made of piss and vinegar. Usually, he could sense it without trouble. With Mackenzie Moore, she reeked of it. The lightly-freckled redhead had something to prove to everybody, and she did it by showing them that she was tougher than she appeared.

Sketchy past, maybe?

Regardless of why, it was a great quality to have—mainly if you spent most of your time in the field surrounded by strangers and dangers. Bones totally understood the attribute, having it himself. There were many beasts in the world that would love to get a taste out of someone like Mack, both human and not.

Then again, there were indeed cannibalistic giants in the world, so both definitions applied to some. They were sort of human, but not, and they'd love to taste Mack—her flesh and blood.

Eyes blurred, Bones recognized Mack by her frock of distorted red hair. She swung something long and thick, connecting with one of the men's stomachs. He keeled over from the blow and was met with a shot to the head by the same, blunt object. Bones shook his head, clearing his vision some, and saw that it was a well-worn baseball bat.

And Mack had just hit a homer with that swing.

Now, there was one more asshole left, the older of the three. Again, shaking the cobwebs away, Bones saw Dudu stepping towards the infected jerkoff, palms up in a non-threatening pose. He was speaking to him in their tongue, one Bones could only decipher a couple of words of.

It sounded like Dudu knew the person, pleading for him to back down. Mack rushed over to Bones as four more uninfected people came to Dudu's aid, also seemingly knowing the aggressor.

"What happened?" Mack asked, helping Bones to his feet. He hadn't even realized that he had gone to one knee. The pain in his back was finally beginning to fade.

Thank, god.

"My back," Bones replied. "Holy hell it burns."

He felt his shirt get pried away and heard an audible gasp from Mack. "Shit, Bones, that looks bad."

"You're telling me, Red." He chuckled softly. "Jagoff must've caught me with a poisoned blade or something." He looked at Mack who shook her head. "No weapon?"

"None," she replied, looking at one of the fallen men. "The only thing I saw them use was their fingernails."

"Nothing else?" he asked, stunned, needing to be sure.

Mack only replied with a silent shake of her head.

Unsure of what to make of the new information, he instead focused on the continued altercation. Dudu and a few of the other local men had backed the deranged, mutated lunatic up against the shore near the boat Bones had come in on. Any sane person would've tried to make a getaway on the crappy, but still very seaworthy vessel.

This guy wasn't sane, though.

Bones watched from forty feet away as his assailant hissed, turned, and leaped into the murky river. Anybody who was anybody knew these waters had all kinds of nasty predators swimming around in them. Piranhas were one of the most famous Amazonian carnivores, followed closely by the largest snake on the planet, the anaconda.

But instead of being eaten by an animal of any kind, the diseased local merely bellowed in rage, releasing all the air from his lungs. Then, he sank. Bones couldn't tell if the guy was swimming out into deeper water or not. Stepping up next to Dudu, they all waited silently for him to surface.

He did a minute and a half later. Face down. Dead. Drowned.

Bones glanced over at Dudu and saw him quietly whispering to himself—a prayer maybe.

"You knew him?" he asked.

Dudu nodded. "My cousin. He disappeared into the jungle over a year ago. I assumed he was dead until now. His eyes—"

"And skin," Mack added.

"And nails," Bones also added, wincing as he tried to rotate his left shoulder. The slash marks rubbed against his shirt, causing them to sting again.

"Something infected these men," Mack said, turning back to the others. The two surviving attackers both laid unconscious in the middle of the street. No one went to check on them either, and Bones knew why. "A natural contagion maybe?"

Bones had seen a lot in his life. This was something else altogether. Whatever did infect these guys, he wasn't so sure it was like any type of disease he had ever encountered before. To him, these guys looked like they were poisoned by something unnatural like they were experimented on.

He glanced at the end of the road. It dead-ended at the big-ass wall. "What's with the wall?"

"Dudu!"

Everyone turned, finding a lone, slightly-disheveled man standing at the base of the blockade. Bones had no idea who he was, but he did notice that the man was white—not a local.

"Igor!" Dudu shouted, running to him.

Bones and Mack's eyes met, and they hurried off behind their guide. The Russian scientist had shown up at a peculiar time. Someone that was as versed in snakes as Dr. Fetisov was could've easily administered a poison if he had the evil within him to do so. Maybe Igor was off the rails and running tests on the poor saps that called Lovely home.

"What's up, Doc?" Bones asked, earning an eye roll from Mack.

"These men…" he replied, panting. It seemed that the good doctor had been running. "I followed them as fast as I could."

"Why," Bones asked, "so you could see the results of your sick experiments? Seriously, bro, not cool."

Igor looked Bones up and down, confused. "My experiments?" His eyes went wide. "No, not at all. I only study the creatures. I don't perform tests of any kind."

"Then why don't you tell us what happened to these men?" Mack asked, pointing to the two in the middle of the road. One had begun to wake but had quickly been subdued and hogtied. The one that Mack had hit with the baseball bat was down for the count, sprawled on his back, spread-eagle.

Igor blew out a long breath. "They are the men that accompanied me to the jungle last week. I believe they were poisoned by some kind of undiscovered venomous serpent."

"The Yacumama?" Bones asked.

The scientist laughed, removing his ballcap. He stroked his full head of gray hair before answering, composing himself a little as he did. "No, this is not that… This is something much worse."

Not the Yacumama? Bones asked himself. He sighed. Why me?

"What then?" Dudu asked, speaking for the first time since greeting Igor.

Igor's eyes looked sad. "I wish I knew. Nothing I have read suggests that this has anything to do with Yacumama, though."

Bones cringed again, getting the attention of Igor. "What is wrong with him?"

Bones shook his head. "It's nothing. I've had a lot worse and survived."

"Like cannibalistic giants?" Mack asked, obviously baiting him.

He groaned and rubbed his face in frustration. "Really? That crap again?"

She smiled and returned her attention to the matter at hand. "One of the infected men cut him," she explained to Igor. "It's not too bad, though."

"Did they use their fingernails or a weapon?"

Bones gave Mack a curious look.

Does he know something?

"Um," she replied, sounding nervous, "their nails."

Igor cursed in Russian. Bones didn't have to speak the language to know when someone was using profanity within it. It was a gift he had.

"This isn't good." He stormed off, moving towards the now awake infected local. "These men, like you, were poisoned by a powerful toxin, one that I have never seen before."

"Hang on, bro," Bones said, grabbing the fifty-something by the shoulder, "I'm infected with this junk too?"

Igor shrugged. "Again, I don't know anything for sure. They," he motioned to snake-men, "were infected from the toxin's source, from what I can tell, a creature I have yet to see since I found the golden river."

"So, there's a chance that the cuts will just hurt like a bitch and not turn me into a big, handsome, albeit, scaly bastard like them?" Bones asked, trying to control himself. He looked at Dudu, remembering his cousin. "No offense, dude."

"Dudu," the guide corrected, not understanding what Bones meant.

"Sure, whatever, bro." Bones looked at Igor. "If I am infected with this stuff, how long do I have before I become like them." He jabbed a finger at the turned men without looking their way. "And I'd really like to not have that happen. It would seriously ruin my plans."

"It's hard to say." Igor tipped his chin at Dudu. "Can you tell us anything about your cousin—before he disappeared?"

Dudu nodded but looked uncomfortable. "Hernao liked to drink and would constantly get lost in the trees looking for the beast's treasure. One time, in one of his drunken stupors, he came back raving about getting attacked by a monster."

"The Yacumama?" Bones asked.

Dudu nodded. "Yes, but everyone thought he just recalled a dream."

"Sounds more like a nightmare," Mack said, getting another uncomfortable look out of Dudu. It was apparent that he didn't like to talk about what happened.

He breathed in deep and continued. "Hernao was a bit of a scoundrel in these parts and couldn't be trusted—so, naturally, no one believed his tale. Everyone knew the legend of the Yacumama, but no one in Lovely had ever actually seen it. It's a legend after all. Anyways, Hernao became so upset at being called a liar that he stormed off to prove what happened."

"He never returned," Igor finished, patting Dudu on the shoulder.

"He went by himself?" Mack asked, shocked.

Dudu nodded, nervous. "Yes, by himself."

Mack glanced at Bones with a raised eyebrow. Bones saw it too. Their Amazonian compatriot knew more than he was divulging. Honestly, at the moment, Bones didn't care. He could always beat it out of him at a later time. Everyone playing nice was more important right now.

The Russian turned to Bones. "This is why I stayed behind in Brazil instead of returning home. I believed what I heard and searched for months before finding the river of gold."

"What's with that anyway?" Bones asked, feeling his skin crawl. All this talk about poisons and mysterious infections was putting him on edge. And considering he was just bloodied by someone carrying the crap…

Igor shrugged. "I believe there is a connection between the people that worship the beast and the gold. I was being hunted after I found the coin I left for Ms. Moore. It's why I also vanished into the jungle. I was hoping to find what I was searching for while also hiding from my pursuers." His face fell. "But it's apparent that the gold was tracked here regardless of my efforts."

"Don't beat yourself up, Doc," Bones said. "You did what you thought was right. There's no way you could've known for sure that they were after the gold and not you."

"Hang on," Mack said, "they can actually track the movement of gold—sense it?"

Igor shrugged once more. "It's just another thing I'm dying to find out."

Bones laughed and slapped the shorter man on the back. "Me too, Doc." He sighed and looked out to the river. "Me too…"

5

Moments after Bones' altercation with the infected trio, a man who passed as the village's chief of police waddled over—sweat-stained shirt and all. Together with his equally drenched "deputy," and both men suspiciously smelling of vodka, they cuffed and dragged the two survivors away, presumably to the Lovely prison.

Sounds like a lovely place…

Bones' trio of lacerations received proper attention—from the snake scientist no less. Igor patched him up, along with some help from Mack who had seemingly seen some pretty nasty injuries in the field. Thankfully, Bones' wounds, while painful, didn't need much more than a couple of thick butterfly bandages each and an injection filled with a cocktail of antibiotics.

And who can forget the godawful rubbing alcohol bath?

Bones couldn't remember ever experiencing such anguish from such an insignificant looking injury. At the time, Bones thought the snake-man used an acid-dipped katana to open his back, digging in and ripping him open like one of the fish at the town's dock. Bones half-expected the same mangy mutt to show up and start gnawing on him too.

Now, they bounced around deeper into the Amazon, riding in a rusted-out Jeep Wrangler. Bones and Mack sat in back, taking in the view through the open top while Dudu and Igor sat up front chatting about what they expected to find, and which way to go.

Leaving Lovely wasn't as hard as he initially thought it would be. The wall had a simple wooden gate that allowed easy access to the trees beyond. It was, in essence, a leaky wall of random pieces of wood, including rotted sections of boats. It looked like the people of Lovely were using everything they could to keep something out. There were even gaps big enough for a grown man to squeeze through, but nothing substantial enough for their giant snake. He figured that's how the three assholes with scales got in.

"Tell me again why we aren't taking the boat further down river?" As much as Bones hated the oversized canoe of a vessel, he'd rather cruise across the glassy surface of the river than get thrown about while traversing over a narrow, slightly overgrown trail.

"Because, Mr. Bones," Igor replied, turning around in his passenger seat, "we have maps for this area if we were to get lost. The river, on the other hand... It splits up and snakes its way into the unknown."

Snakes... Ha, ha, ha. Bones rolled his eyes. The snake guy said 'snakes.'

"And the routes we do have, do not run near the most recent sightings," Dudu added, yelling while facing forward. "There are no guarantees in what we will find in the waters past Lovely. This is much safer."

The Jeep bucked, jarring Bones' lower back hard. He cringed and shifted in his seat as a branch just missed his head. "Yeah, much safer," he mumbled, ducking lower in his seat.

Happy that nothing had tried to kill them...yet...Bones shifted his attention to the surrounding landscape, taking it all in. There was a calming beauty to the jungle most of the time, minus when something was, in fact, trying to eat him. Seriously, he didn't know anyone who got into more misadventures than him.

No time for that... Pity parties weren't something Bones included himself in. Unless they included a seven-foot-tall, singing clown named "Puddles." He smiled to himself. That dude can sing.

The trees were lush—healthy. They stretched on forever, which wasn't too far from the truth. The Amazon, while shrinking daily due to deforestation, was still massive in size. Bones didn't much care for how big the rainforest was precisely, but he knew it was an impressive number either way. The fact that only a small portion of it had even been explored and mapped lent to the jungle's girth and inaccessibility.

The Jeep bucked again. Including over land. He rubbed his back. Ow.

Then again, Igor and Dudu did just warn him about the jungle's rivers and their tendency to "snake" their way through the terrain. Even the most knowledgeable of people—real experts on the Amazon—would easily get lost, never to be heard from or seen again. Even Bones wasn't foolish enough to run headlong into a place like this. He'd rely on their guide, a local man, even if his name really was "Dudu."

"I came this way originally," Igor explained. "Myself and the two younger men from town. This road ends just up ahead, turning into an impasse of trees and muck."

"So," Bones said, "we're hoofing it then?"

Igor nodded. "Yes, unfortunately."

"How long?" Mack asked, getting to the question before Bones could.

"We should be back in Lovely in two days if we're

quick."

"That's it?" Mack asked. "I thought our destination would be more remote than that?"

Igor snickered. "Two days is remote out here, Ms. Moore. You could be a half a mile away from civilization and never know it."

Bones leaned back in his seat, cursing under his breath. Two days of romping through the jungle with people he had just met didn't sound like a good time to him. Thankfully, his company all seemed to have level heads about them. No one would be going crazy from "jungle madness" anytime soon.

"It is here," Dudu announced, slowing the Jeep.

Bones and Mack both leaned in between the seats in front of them, getting awkwardly close to one another in the process. It's not that Bones didn't find the redhead attractive—she was undeniably pleasant to look at. It was that she was his employer and her focus was on the job…not him. Bones had always had success with the ladies over the years, but he could see from the time he met Mack, even without the fist to his jaw, that she was off-limits.

Too bad.

"Great…" Bones exhaled and stood.

Mack did the same except she left the confines of the vehicle and dropped down to the moist soil below. Everything in the Amazon was wet. Bones was going to survey the area from above, in the relative safety of the Jeep. Dudu could shift to reverse and get them out of here in a pinch if something went wrong. Now, with one of their teammates exposed, Bones was forced to join her.

But before he did, Bones snagged an ax from the rear of the Jeep, hefting it onto his shoulder like a lumberjack.

It would be perfect for clearing large debris that a machete couldn't chop through.

It also reminded Bones of his and Maddock's visit to Norway. They were both involved in a skirmish inside a Viking-inspired sporting goods store. The entire left-hand wall of the place was stocked with axes, like how you'd see fishing poles at other stores. That's how they were stocked around where he lived in Key West.

Patting his thigh, Bones unconsciously felt for the Glock that was usually holstered there and readily available when needed. He didn't like to take any chances while out in the wild. If it weren't for the three snake-men, Bones would've felt just fine without it. But since they showed up and acted rudely, Bones was on high-alert until further notice, wishing he had anything that threw lead.

Plus, he really enjoyed swinging an ax around. It was an excellent change-of-pace weapon for him. He wished he had one of the "special" axes from Norway, though. Those things were truly out-of-this-world.

"Why has no one come here before?" Bones asked quietly, looking around. "I mean, it's not that far from civilization."

"Besides the two days of Amazonian hiking," Mack reminded him.

"Besides that," Bones agreed. He shook his head, shoulders slumping. "Thanks for reminding me, Red."

"Stop calling me that!" she hissed, earning shushes from everyone. She shrugged and whispered. "What?"

Bones tapped his left ear. The look on her face was instantaneous. There was no sound at all. Nothing. No jungle in the world was this quiet. Either something was upon them, or the creatures that called this leg of the Amazon home knew not to venture here.

Just perfect.

Dudu and Igor stayed in the Jeep while Bones and Mack searched for anything suspicious. Bones laughed inwardly. They were in a rainforest. Everything in a rainforest was suspect to a degree.

"Psst."

Bones glanced over to Mack who had moved farther off than he would've liked. She was thirty feet ahead of him, standing on one of the fallen trees that blocked the path. The tree was large and looked like it had been there for some time. Different types of vines and other stringy plants had grown all over it, securing it further. There were a few more trees down on the other side too, adding to the natural blockade.

Something had come through in years past and unrooted them. Nothing else in the area was disturbed. So, what could've done it? *A big-ass snake, that's what!*

Gripping his ax tighter, Bones headed for the adventurous journalist. She seemed to be perfectly comfortable out in the world, jotting down notes as she moved. Her confident, borderline reckless, actions made Bones smile a little. He wouldn't have to be watching her back every second of every minute. She would make his job easier and allow Bones to focus on their task entirely.

"Look."

He followed her extended finger. Attached to the nearest log was something that looked like snakeskin. Only, it was gold. Lifting his ax higher, Bones did a quick three-sixty, keeping the weapon gripped tightly in his hands. Their beast had been here recently, rubbing up against the fallen tree on its way through.

That got Dudu and Igor's attention. Both men came rushing forward, weapons in hand. Each held a machete as they approached, scanning their surroundings like a pair of barn owls—heads of swivels. Bones was impressed that they took in the land around them as well as they did. Mack did the same too, never keeping her eyes off the terrain for too long. Of course, all of them had spent some time in places like this at one time or another. It becomes habit to watch your ass when something wants to take a chunk out of it.

"Oh, my." It was all Igor could say before diving into his pack. He quickly procured a small specimen jar and a pair of tweezers. With practiced patience and a steady hand, he plucked the six-inch-long piece of gleaming skin from the log. "Unbelievable."

"Nothing is unbelievable."

From his kneeling position, Igor looked up at Bones. He didn't question him, though, only nodding and looking away with a far-off look in his eyes. The snake expert was thinking, and thinking hard. His brain was in overdrive trying to deduce what they had discovered.

"What are you thinking, Doc?" Bones asked, facing away from the others. He knelt and inspected the path a few feet in front of the barricade. There was definitely something there—in addition to the ground itself. It was in the ground, actually.

"Well, damn…"

Someone took a knee beside him, but Bones was too entranced with the tracks to look. He rubbed his hand across the depressions, amazed at their depth and overall size. Whatever it was, Yacumama or not, it was enormous.

Igor was next to inspect the tracks, hopping over them to the other side. He spoke softly to himself, naturally switching to his first language, Russian. "This is definitely not the giant anaconda I came here to study."

He glanced up at Bones. "This is something else."

"Yacumama?" Mack asked.

"No," Dudu said from behind, not getting any closer. Even someone scared out of their mind would want to see the tracks. Dudu looked almost disinterested. "There are no stories of it being gold. Like Igor has said, this is something else."

He's hiding something, Bones thought. *He knows more.*

"Its size is troublesome too," Igor continued. He bit his lip, obviously doing the calculations in his head. "From the depth of the creature's tracks and their width, our snake must be upwards of eighty feet long—maybe more."

"Holy crap," Bones muttered. It wasn't the 125 feet the Yacumama was said to be, but it was still a behemoth. Which begged the question. "How does something that big, and gold, stay hidden for this long?"

"And what does it eat?" Mack added.

Igor stood, prompting Bones and Mack to do the same. "Some of the larger anaconda within the Amazon have been known to take down caimans with relative ease. Plus, most of the larger species only live to around ten years old in the wild. I've heard of a few surviving into their late teens, but nothing more. For something to grow to this size, it would have to be…"

"Thirty?" Bones asked, guesstimating.

Igor shook his head. "Ancient. There's no telling how old our friend is."

"There's more," Mack said, tipping her chin to their left.

Bones immediately saw them. There, side by side with the monster's tracks were smaller depressions. The gate, size, and shape were unmistakable.

"People?" Bones muttered. "There were people were traveling with the creature."

"Maybe they were running from it," Dudu said. "We do not know that they were accompanying it."

Bones turned and looked up at him, raising a single eyebrow. "After what we saw with the three punks back in Lovely, the evidence would suggest the opposite. It's pretty obvious that this thing has friends out here."

"Plus," Mack said, "these footprints indicate that their owners were walking, not running." She pointed to the gap in between them. "The spacing is all wrong if someone was running for their life. The weight should be on the balls of their feet too, not evenly distributed."

While impressed with Mack's ability to correctly diagnose the human prints, Bones wasn't thinking about them anymore. He was thinking of the men that had attacked him. Were they the ones traveling alongside their, what, god?

If not, then how many more people are worshiping the beast, and where is their civilization? In his mind's eye, and with a little boyish imagination, Bones pictured the scene. An ancient city is hidden somewhere within the Amazon. The people living there, whether by choice or not, believed the imposter-Yacumama to be their living deity, the one from their local legend. But for that to happen, and for human beings to peacefully coexist with a giant snake, it meant that the snake itself held some sort of higher-functioning intelligence. It would be able to interact with them on a social level.

Bones sighed. *This just keeps getting better and better.*

6

Back at the hut-bar-lounge, Bones was still stunned that Igor wanted to return to town instead of continuing the pursuit of their prize. He babbled on about needing more time to prepare and wanting to contact a few of his colleagues around the globe. He said he had a fairly modern satellite hookup in his makeshift office above the lounge and required some time to get a proper signal.

There were only a couple of rooms there, and Bones was happy to find out that he had one of them. But he'd be bunking with Mack.

This shouldn't be awkward or anything.

He dropped off his stuff before heading back down the creaking, outdoor stairs. His and Mack's room was small, but thankfully, not too small. It had one tiny mattress, and it was on the floor with no box spring. It was honestly more than Bones expected to see. He figured that the room would be just four walls with a ceiling and floor complete with matching holes. How the place didn't collapse in on itself was beyond his understanding of architecture.

Even an outdoor tent would've done just fine considering where they were. Bones didn't anticipate there actually being buildings in Lovely. Most small villages along the Amazon river system were handmade huts of leaves and logs. While some of those dotted the small main road, there were some structures made from plywood and drywall.

Must've cost a fortune to import.

Bones almost laughed when he found out that Dudu owned and operated the dockside watering hole. His mother ran it with him and was in charge when he did his tour guide thing. Apparently, their family had what was considered "wealth" in these parts. How or why wasn't Bones' concern. He chalked it up to good business, and/or good fortune.

Bones had a ton of both in his lifetime. He was good at what he did and had a lot of good luck along the way. Mostly not dying when he probably should've... Not wanting to reflect on all of his near misses, Bones leaned back in his seat and waited for Igor to return.

Mack sat across from him, looking through her notes, mumbling to herself. She'd occasionally jot down something new, her eyebrows creasing inward as she did. Mack would also bite her lip while she wrote, looking very cute while she did it. If she had pigtails and overalls, Mack would look like your prototypical country tomboy. The light freckling on her face added to the imagery. There weren't many of them, but the tiny, sprinkles of color seemed to be precisely applied to the right spots. A couple on her cheeks. A few on her nose. One on her chin.

Dudu was off somewhere, and like Igor, he was chatting it up with the local populace. He wanted to see what he could dig up on their little problem—see if anyone had seen anything and not reported it. It didn't matter how long ago it was either.

Bones wanted to know everything about their creature, even if it sounded utterly ridiculous and impossible. He excelled in the impossible. Any information relating to a giant golden snake would be taken as truth considering what they just found.

Gold snakeskin.

"What are the chances that the golden river that Igor saw wasn't actually the water," his eyes found Mack's, "but our snake submerged beneath the surface? Depending on its true size and that of the river's too, of course."

Mack nodded. "I was thinking the same. It would make sense since Igor couldn't find it again." She shrugged. "He probably did but since it wasn't gold the next time he saw it, he didn't recognize it for what it was. And," Mack continued, "the rivers and banks throughout the rainforest would look identical to one another if you weren't overly familiar with the area." She shrugged. "Could've been a narrow stream for all we know. Igor's English is exceptional, but he may've originally meant stream, not river." She shook her head and scribbled out something in her notes. "A lot of maybes..."

"I agree." Bones said. "He probably passed by the exact spot several times. I can imagine his frustration."

"What of the coin then?" Mack asked.

"That's easy..." Bones replied, sitting forward, "we saw footprints with the serpent's tracks. One of the people following along with it could've easily dropped it while climbing over the downed trees."

"They had pockets?" Mack asked, smirking.

Bones laughed at the silliness of his statement. "The dudes we encountered, they were wearing modern clothing. It's possible the ones following the snake had similar clothes on as well. We aren't talking about a tribe of naked natives here. These are—were—normal, everyday people at one point, from villages that had seen plenty of interaction with outsiders like us."

"Slaves?" Mack asked.

"It's possible, but toxins and the way they affect the brain aren't my forte. Let's see what Igor says after talking to his buddies back in the motherland."

Mack bit her lip once more but nodded.

Then, a second chorus of screams rang out.

Now what?

Bones and Mack could only look at one another before darting to the door, weapons at the ready. Neither one of them were taking any chances. Bones still had his ax and Mack a machete. Not bothering to stop and open the flimsy, balsa wood door, Bones blew through it instead, shouldering it off its meek hinges. It sailed out into the late-afternoon sun, clattering across the densely compacted dirt road that ran down the center of Lovely.

Wincing, Bones regretted using his injured shoulder to ram the door. Pain lanced up and down his arm as well as his back, stopping at his ass. If he had been holding the ax in his left hand, he would've surely dropped it. The jolt caused his fingers to spasm open for a split second.

A grinding sound caught his attention. It came from his left, further down the main road, toward the wall. He looked just in time to see the hodgepodgery of a barricade get blown to bits, exploding towards him in a shower of wooden shrapnel. There, emerging from the destruction, and in all its horrible glory, was their monster.

And it was a lot bigger than their initial assessment.

Bones was amazed when it reared up, its head over twenty feet in the air by the time it finished. It had arched the front portion of its body up like a cobra, getting a bird's eye view of the now tiny looking village. Lovely wasn't the smallest place Bones had ever seen, but it wasn't big either. Seeing the creature's girth alongside the modest-sized, wood-framed buildings, Bones was too stunned to move.

And it was most definitely gold.

Its underbelly was the same milky-gold color as the asses who attacked Bones earlier in the afternoon. The rest of it, however, was a brilliant, lustrous gold. The setting sun reflected off it like a beacon to the primeval gods, making the thing look like it was glowing from with—

Hang on, Bones thought. The sun is too low for it to be causing that.

He looked closer.

"It's emitting the glow internally?" Mack asked aloud, unsure, but on the same wavelength as Bones.

"Hot damn," he mumbled, gripping his ax harder.

So far, the snake seemed to be cautiously taking in the village. It appeared unsure of what to make of Lovely. It had only moved in a little further than the tree line, keeping the rest of its size hidden in the shadows of the thick canopy of leaves beyond the shattered gate.

Hot damn...

The word 'hot' usually referred to someone, or something's, temperature, but it also was used when describing whether something was radioactive or not. Is that what this is? Bones couldn't be sure of anything at the moment, but maybe, just maybe, their monster was the result of the undisclosed dumping of radioactive material.

He glanced up at the sky and thought of another possible culprit. Alien tech? It, again, wasn't a long shot. Few people around the globe knew as much about aliens living on Earth like he did. There was loads of evidence to support it, but the findings were, as expected, swept under the rug by various governmental organizations.

Some were friendly to Bones and Maddock.

Most weren't.

Bones was putting his money on the mutation angle, natural or not, but a type of undiscovered alien technology in the Amazon was a close second. Hopefully, it was a mutation. He'd hate to have to explain it all to Mack. There was no way he'd be able to keep his intimate knowledge of beings from outer space to himself if they found E.T. out here.

The beast opened its hideous mouth slightly, resonating a sound like grinding stone. Its hiss was what Bones and Mack heard earlier, just before it obliterated the gate and parts of the wall.

"Well," Bones said, "that's not terrifying or anything."

Even as scared as he was, Bones' mind was working through every conceivable scenario. After a dozen or so, he concluded that this thing could, and most likely would, lay waste to Lovely. If Godzilla was a snake, this was the moment it was waiting for.

Smash, roar in anger, smash, roar in anger...and so on.

Bones backed away slowly, pulling Mack along. "We need to leave."

"But—"

"No buts, Red," Bones interrupted, getting her attention with the nickname she hated. "This," he held up the ax, "is going to do jack squat to that." He pointed at the creature.

It was looking right at them. Its eyes squinted, and its head tilted slightly. It was acting like a dog trying to understand its master.

It was showing intelligence.

"Oh, damn…"

The serpent's head was longer and thicker too, giving it an almost crocodilian appearance. And with its mouth agape, Bones could clearly see two huge fangs accompanied by twin rows of serrated, blade-like teeth.

Bones and Mack froze in place, but Bones knew it wouldn't matter how good or bad the thing's eyesight was. All snakes had an impeccable sense of smell, and this one was no different, flicking its long, black tongue in and out of its mouth, tasting the air.

Its eyes, like everything else, were proportionately huge. They also sported golden irises. There was little doubt that the creature was the source of the snake-men's virus, the one Bones now most likely carried. As much as Bones wanted gold eyes—and let's be honest, who wouldn't—he'd really, really like to not become one of this thing's underlings.

Six men appeared beside the serpent king, all in various stages of transformation. Two of them, presumably the ones exposed the longest, wore no clothes and sported entire bodies covered in golden scales. The other guys wore clothes like Dudu's cousin.

The recently turned, Bones thought.

The snake made its move, launching its entire girth down the short dirt road. It moved impossibly fast for its size, slithering like your average snake did. Over a hundred feet later, the tip of its tail appeared, giving everyone watching the first real glimpse at what was believed to be the mythological Yacumama.

They watched in horror as its body involuntarily coiled around a small building and squeezed. The structure imploded from the dynamic force of the behemoth, sending out multiple sets of screams from within.

What was also interesting, besides the raw power it displayed, was that the snake had spines running down the length of its back, giving it a feathered appearance. It reminded Bones of the Maya legend of Kukulkan. The ancient Mesoamerican god's name literally translated to "feathered serpent." It was also the name of the famous pyramid dedicated to the deity at Chichen Itza.

El Castillo, Bones thought. *AKA, Kukulkan's Pyramid.*

He looked the monster over again, seeing it for what it was. It looked remarkably like the carvings depicted in every ancient Mesoamerican culture. Plumed snakes could be found all over Central America, some even being found in South America.

Bones didn't think the creature in front of him was the inspiration behind the Maya's lore, but maybe this thing was related to a serpent that was? It was a question for another time.

"Move!" he shouted, shoving Mack aside. Together, they ran back toward Dudu's place. Bones knew full well that the sheer walls had no shot of keeping the Yacumama at bay, but it was easily the sturdiest of them all.

Gotta figure out another name for this golden prick too.

They slipped into the hole that was just recently the front door, the one Bones destroyed a few minutes prior. When they did, the wall encompassing the opening was annihilated by something huge. Bones looked over his shoulder in time to see an enormous gold blur shred the building, shaking the structure horribly as it did. The roof above his and Mack's head, the second level's floor, creaked and snapped.

"Holy shit!" Mack yelled, flinching as the ceiling splintered, raining dust and grime on them.

They could hear Igor above them yelling, shouting in fright. He was still upstairs in the middle of calling his colleagues in Russia. He was going to come down with the rest of the place if he didn't get out of his room in time.

"We need to help him!" Bones shouted.

He stepped toward the back door, intent on leaping up the stairs if he had to. Instead, Mack grabbed his arm and spun him around the other way. Four of the recently arrived snake-men stepped in and stopped, standing at attention.

"I'll get Igor," Mack said, patting his shoulder. "You stay here and entertain the guests."

7

Before he could argue with her, Mack disappeared outside, leaving Bones alone with four very angry looking mutants. He calmly cracked his neck, unsheathed his knife, and threw it at the nearest enemy, striking him in the chest, dropping him. The other three jumped into motion, moving like the trio that attacked Bones earlier.

He swung the ax back and forth, clipping two of them, before having to go on the defensive, blocking a bevy of slashes and fingernail jabs. Losing the ax, Bones grabbed a nearby wooden stool, and slammed it into the next guy, stumbling him into another. The chair's legs came free in Bones' hands, and he used them like police batons when attacked again.

One of the snake-men overextended himself with a wild swipe, tripping on the remains of the busted stool. Bones dropped one of the batons and gripped onto the back of the dude's shirt. Using his momentum against him, Bones shoved the guy headfirst into the rear wall. The snake-man hit hard and collapsed in on himself.

Two more.

The ceiling gave again, and split straight down the middle, left to right. Then, the side of the building closest to the road began to list. Bones glanced up and then back to his foes. They slowly stalked forward, moving in unison with one another. It was the same behavior as the others. He reacted by backing away.

They don't care that they're about to get crushed!

An explosion erupted overhead, and so did two sets

of shrill cries. Bones leaped back and looked up again, just in time to see Mack dive through the widening crack in the floor above. She was running from something, and Bones saw what it was when he looked beyond the remaining snake-men. The Yacu-whatever was back, driving its head through Igor's window.

Mack fell like a bomb, barely squeezing through the opening overhead, landing hard on both of Bones' foes. It would've been comical, but Bones was too frightened for Mack. What if she also got infected? Helping her up, Bones balled his right fist and—

No one else got up.

Mack knocked them out cold when she crashed down atop them like a human-sized sack of potatoes.

"Well, that was effective," Bones said, laughing, coughing.

Mack wasn't having it, though. "Igor's gone."

"What?" Bones asked, not sure what she meant.

"Gone as in dead, or gone as in, you know, gone?"

"I don't know," she yelled, "both?"

The room came apart around them. The two of them had to dodge falling debris, unable to get to the rear exit. Broken two-by-fours and drywall blocked it now. Only, they couldn't go out the front either. The giant snake was still outside, presumably looking for them, preventing them from escaping into town.

"What do you mean both?" Bones asked, hugging Mack into his chest. He'd protect her if he could. So far, the ceiling directly above their heads had stayed together. It seemed that Bones still had a little luck left after all.

"When it came through the window," she shouted against the cacophony, not pushing away from him, "it unhinged its jaw and swallowed Igor whole."

"What!" Bones replied, looking up.

He couldn't believe what he was hearing, and that he missed it to boot. As terrible as it was that the snake ate Igor, Bones would've loved to have seen the creature in action.

And why only the Russian?

At that very second, while the second floor crumbled around them, it didn't matter. The only thing that did was Bones and Mack staying alive long enough to formally ask the question.

With one final snap, the front-half of the building gave up and fell. Surprisingly, the other half, the half above Bones and Mack, stayed erect. Just inside the break, they watched in almost slow motion. Dudu's place was no more, as was the much smaller building across the road. It was smashed to pieces by the two-story façade.

Bones found his ax readied it, but didn't see the serpent—or any of the snake-men.

"Where'd everyone go?" he asked more to himself. He became furious. "How does something that freaking big just vanish?"

A bang to their right caused Bones to whirl around. His sights were set on…Dudu. Bones had almost killed the man as he stumbled inside, a little twitchy from what had just happened. It's not every day that an oversized, shiny anaconda wreaks a building with you in it.

Bones stretched his back. Sometimes feels like it, though.

Dudu threw his hands up, a look of shock on his face. His place of business being destroyed must've been too much for him to handle and he fainted. Bones didn't bother helping the unconscious man either. He had other things to do first.

"What about Dudu?" Mack asked.

"What about him?"

Mack glanced at the prone guide and then looked back at Bones. "I guess he'll be okay, right?"

Bones smiled. "Just like taking a nap," he glanced up, "underneath a crumbling structure built in the Amazon." Talking himself out of not helping Dudu, Bones moved towards him. "You know what, I think we should at least move him out of the way. We can't have our guide get squished by his own building, can we?"

"No, we can't," Mack replied, rolling her eyes. She grabbed Dudu's ankles and lifted.

Back near the smallish dock, Bones and Mack laid Dudu on the bench they sat on earlier that afternoon. Bones needed to see if he could find any evidence to as why Igor was killed, or maybe taken, and not them too. He was holding out hope that the Russian was still alive somehow, but after what Mack had described, Bones was leaning towards him being dead. Snake food.

"Try and wake him, will ya?" Bones asked, heading off. "I'm going to see what I can find."

Mack nodded and slapped Dudu in the face a few times, harder than Bones would've guessed. Flinching at the series of strikes, Bones rubbed his chin, feeling a slight pressure beneath his fingers. She had hit him pretty damn hard. It didn't exactly hurt, but it was sore.

Climbing atop the still-shifting wreckage, Bones carefully made his way over the broken remains. The only way up to the now ultra-spacious room with a view was to scale a large pile of wood and glass. There was no concrete in these parts. Everything was made of wood, most of it weak and rotten from years of exposure. Piece after piece splintered or bowed beneath his weight, but luckily, Bones still made some headway.

He was now directly under the missing section to Igor's room. Bones grabbed onto a somewhat intact support beam, one that had just recently been holding the roof together, and hauled himself higher. He used every foot and handhold he could find, even using the busted-out window frame as a step. The creature had hit it so hard that it literally popped free of the wall, keeping it mostly in one piece—minus the glass. It was currently jammed between Igor's mattress and a random section of flooring.

Half-climbing, half-leaping, Bones made it up to Igor's decimated room, rolling onto the floor with a hard bang. His added weight caused the remaining structure to shudder beneath him, groaning like a sick two-story tall cow. He needed to move fast or else he'd end up like Igor's wall. For good measure, he tried to open the Russian's door but found it blocked.

No going that way.

Luckily for Bones, there was only half a room to search, and he combed the place the best he could. There was wood and glass everywhere, and Lord knows he'd need a couple of tetanus shots if he cut himself on something.

Bones lifted a piece of the ceiling away from the floor with his foot and found a piece of paper with some writing on it. Thankfully, it was in English and not Russian. They'd be SOL if it were the other way around.

The note was chaotic—random. Words like venom and evil were written next to others like natural and ancient. Even more words were smeared and illegible. It seemed that Igor and his colleagues were leaning toward a naturally occurring mutation from what Bones could tell. There wasn't any mention of extraterrestrials or even that of scientific studies or experimentation. Bones wouldn't have been the least bit surprised if someone mentioned a secret lab somewhere out in the Amazon.

The only people that could pull it off would be a company like ScanoGen, but they usually showed up after something was found. They had been a pain in Bones' ass for some time, but this didn't fit their M.O. Typically, the Scano family tried to acquire new tech and/or biologics to make weapons with, selling their wares to the highest bidder. They had, unfortunately, shown up in Norway at the same time he and Maddock did.

What about ICE? Bones asked himself.

The Initiative for Control of Extraterrestrials was a shadowy organization that he had encountered in New Mexico while searching for the famed "Book of Bones." No relation... No one had heard from ICE since, though. Not even Tam and her CIA contacts. They had fallen entirely off the radar after the events surrounding Halcon Rock. Bones didn't even know if ICE still existed, but if this gold snake had anything to do with aliens, the people running the group would almost certainly know about it.

"Find anything?"

Bones turned and looked down to ground level. Mack was standing beneath his perch, hands on hips, looking tired. He was really impressed with the way she carried herself, even in the face of something as terrifying as the serpent and its minions.

"Just some notes—nothing we haven't already gone over." He tossed the page aside and undid his ponytail, quickly retying it. Lifting his shoulder hurt, but it wasn't anything he couldn't push through. "I'm still trying to wrap my head around why Igor was attacked and not us."

Mack laughed. "Um, we were attacked," she pointed

to a foot protruding from beneath the rubble, "remember?"

Bones shook his head. "Not them…it. Why didn't the monster pursue us further after it went after the good doctor? What made him so special?"

Mack patted her pockets, her chin dropping after not finding what she wanted. "The coin… I gave it to Igor to study."

Bones stomped the ground hard. "Dammit! Again, with that coin!"

The floor came loose beneath Bones, and he plummeted straight through, yelping when he did. For a moment, he thought he'd fall forever. That moment ended when he crashed through a table, slamming into the hardwood floor. He groaned, unable, and not wanting, to move. He had only been in Lovely for a few hours and was already sick of the place. Footsteps announced the arrival of Mack who snickered as she slid into view.

"See something funny, Red?" he asked, not seeing the humor in what just happened.

Still on his back, Bones brushed off his clothes, lifting his head high enough to see her nod. "Your face when the floor gave out. Priceless."

Holding out a hand, Mack helped him to his feet. Bones rolled his neck and stretched his lower back. "So is that coin yours, apparently. Must be some kind of sacred token or something. What the heck is so special about it?"

"Bones?"

"Yeah?" he replied, climbing over another pile of debris, making his way back outside.

"What do we do now?"

He didn't answer her until he was back out in the

middle of the road. Bones was happy to see Dudu on his feet, holding his head while he talked to a woman and her distraught son. Turning back toward the end of the road, Bones smiled.

"What?" Mack asked, not seeing it.

"Our friend left in a hurry."

A portion of the tree line at the end of the main road was flattened. The creature had rushed back into the jungle after attacking Igor. To Bones, it seemed that it got what it wanted with the coin. Igor had only been in the way, probably carrying it in his pocket like Mack had been doing.

He looked at Mack and grinned. "We're going on the hunt."

8

They left the Jeep at the downed trees, right where they found the gold snakeskin. The vehicle's front tires were actually parked atop Goldilocks' tracks. Bones decided that "Yacumama" wasn't the right name for the creature. The spines across its back sort of looked like thick pieces of hair, so the new name fit.

Bones now had his own machete, along with a recently acquired pistol, a Taurus PT-92, and another combat knife. His own knife was still buried in the chest of one of the snake-men beneath a pile of rubble.

Mack was given an upgrade over the machete, though she still carried one. Dudu also gave her a Taurus PT-92. The handguns were standard issue in the Brazilian military, and something he wasn't supposed to have.

Apparently, Dudu did some illegal trading on the side as well owning a "bed and breakfast." The guide also had his own upgrade in weaponry. Found all over the world, the Soviet-made Kalashnikov assault rifle, more commonly known as an AK47, hung around his back as they marched forward.

Another weapon he isn't supposed to have. He gripped his gun. Not that I really care right now.

Bones knew that Brazil had some pretty strict gun laws, hence why he didn't have his favorite gun, his Glock. He wanted to bring it but had done a little research on the subject before leaving Florida. The risk wasn't worth it.

"She went this way," Bones said, kneeling before more of the creature's tracks.

"She?" Mack asked eyebrow raised.

"Goldilocks is a girl, right?" Calling the monster a she didn't feel right. Bones decided that from now on the thing was an it.

He moved off before Mack could question him again. Goldi's trail was an easy one to follow. It had continued down the opposite side of the overgrown path, the one the Jeep couldn't traverse. Bones and Mack had their personal packs with them while Dudu carried their supplies, camping equipment included. He was essentially their pack mule. He didn't seem to care, however. After the serpent ruined his livelihood, the local man wanted revenge.

"You still with us, bro?" Bones asked.

He nodded. "We can rebuild, but not with this demon living so close by. It needs to die before Lovely can rebuild."

"Down, boy," Bones said, looking at Mack.

"He's right," Mack said. "Lives are in jeopardy—a whole village."

He waved her off. "I know. I just don't want the only person in our trio that knows the terrain to go nuts and ditch us because of a deathwish. I'd hate to never go home." He stopped and rubbed his shoulder. "Unless J.Lo is out here somewhere looking for the same snake…" He smiled. "That would be worth staying for."

"Who is J.Lo?" Dudu asked.

Bones groaned and rubbed his forehead. "She's a singer-actress and starred in a movie about a giant anaconda in the Amazon?" Blank stare from Dudu. "She's currently banging A-Rod? Ring any bells?"

"What's an A-Rod?"

"You know what," Bones half-shouted, fed up,

"never mind. Forget I said anything. Let's rewind to the part where you were going mental and go from there."

"Shhh…"

Mack hushed him, and before he could retaliate, he understood why. The jungle around them was deathly silent, like before. Whatever critters called this part of the rainforest home had abandoned it when Goldilocks came through. The trio followed its trail as it veered left, off the trail and into the brush.

Off the beaten path.

"I need to tell you something before we venture further," Dudu said, getting Bones and Mack's attention. They stopped and waited for the local to continue. "I talked with a few of the elders. After witnessing the creature lay waste to Lovely, they started rambling on about something disturbing."

"And that is…" Bones wanted the guy to cut to the chase.

"The Sachamama," Dudu replied.

"The what?" Mack asked.

Dudu's face fell. "The 'earth mother.'"

Bones heard him, but his mind was already leaping ahead. The coin Igor found, the one that had most likely cost him his life… It had two snakes on it.

"On the coin," Bones said. "The earth mother and the water mother." He looked at Mack. "There are two of these bastards out here, aren't there?"

Dudu shrugged. "Only a handful of the elders had heard of a golden serpent before—many, many years ago. The Sachamama is a legend, like the Yacumama, but far less known. It had been generations since anyone had heard anything about it, though. People stopped telling its stories after a while." He pointed at his chest. "Even I needed to be reminded of it by the oldest of our people."

"But we haven't seen another giant snake," Mack said, earning nods from both men.

"Yet," Bones added. "The coin has two snakes. It's reasonable to think that there is, or at least was another one."

"So, best-case scenario, the Yacumama might be long dead." Mack was worried but tried to be hopeful.

"Sure, it's possible, but it's also possible that we haven't seen it yet. Whoever made that coin believes in the pair living at the same time."

"At this point," Dudu said, "you have to believe in their being two of them. One being real was already unfathomable. Two should not be such a stretch."

"Should be quite a story, huh Red?"

Mack glanced at Bones, silently nodding. He noticed that she wasn't currently taking notes, and he asked as much.

"Why aren't you recording any of this?" He raised an eyebrow.

"You were jotting down notes like a madwoman back in town. Why not here?" His eyes opened wider. "Don't tell me you have some sort of photographic memory or something?"

She smiled. "No, I don't have a photographic memory, though it is pretty damn good." Her voice broke a little. "I can't imagine writing a story while we're searching for a missing member of our team, especially if it's his body." She shook her head. "Doesn't seem right, or responsible. Besides," she held up her drawn pistol, "I've got my hands full right now."

The trio hiked for another two hours before settling down for the night. They decided to camp with a fire blazing, hoping that the heat and light would ward off any visitors. Typically, snakes were attracted to heat. Bones prayed that their beast wasn't.

Bones quickly announced that he'd take first watch, letting the emotionally unbalanced Dudu and the mentally fractured Mack rest. Mack, like Bones, would never admit it, but she was shaken up good. Dudu didn't have to admit anything. His mania was out in the open, plain to see.

They had gotten lucky back in Lovely. No one, except Igor, was harmed. Even the villagers survived the battle, fleeing the center of town as soon as the monster revealed itself. Bones and Mack had taken out four of the snake-men without losing anyone else. Two of Goldilocks' minions, the ones that didn't engage, disappeared along with the Sachamama herself. Bones decided the it was a "she" for sure. It was called the "earth mother" after all, and his reservations about calling it a chick earlier were gone.

But he wasn't going to verbally call it a female. No chance in hell.

"So," Bones said, thinking aloud, "if both of our snakes are chicks, are we to assume that the species doesn't reproduce the old-fashioned way?" He made a circle with the forefinger and thumb of his left hand and then aggressively rammed the pointer finger on his right hand through the makeshift hole. For added effect, he flicked his eyebrows several times.

"Are we sure that they reproduce at all?" Mack replied, asking her own question. "And that was such a nice thing to open my eyes too." She mimicked his "reproductive" hand gesture.

Propped up against a tree, Mack had just awoken,

eyes still droopy. She stretched and then yawned, rubbing her eyes, still tired from her catnap. Looking down at his watch, Bones confirmed the time. It was Mack's turn to keep an eye on their asses, and his time to sleep.

Fat chance.

"What are you thinking?" he asked, wanting to see where Mack was taking this.

She leaned forward and wrapped her arms around her knees, staring into the small fire. Bones had tended to it while the others slept.

"If what Igor said was true," she said, "then these creatures are most likely hundreds of years old. He called them 'ancient.'" She looked hard into Bones' eyes. "You more than anyone can attest to there being some strange things out in the world."

Bones knew she was talking about Cabras. If Mack was one thing, it was persistent. He already knew she was someone he could be honest with, but the stuff he knew needed to stay on the down low for a good reason. Most people, even Bones, would be scared shitless of the things he had seen and experienced. Knowledge was power, and there were some awful people in the world that would love to acquire such knowledge.

"Two immortal," he said the word with finger quotes, "extra-large snakes wouldn't be the weirdest thing I've seen." She raised an eyebrow. "Take my word for it."

Mack nodded. "I believe you." She smiled. "I just want to hear you say it."

"Say what?" He grinned back.

"That you fought giants in Cabras."

He winked. "Never gonna happen, Red."

They sat in silence, both looking hard at the fire. Mack was the next one to speak, continuing the conversation about the snakes being immortal.

"If they are impossible to kill, how'd it happen?"

Bones laughed. "Just because they're immortal, doesn't mean they're impossible to kill. Greenland sharks don't reach maturity until they're 150 years old. They literally don't age at all—well, hardly at all, anyways. There was this scientist dude who studied a living specimen that was said to be over 400 years old, and it was in perfect health."

"So," Mack said, "maybe our snakes aren't technically immortal. Maybe they just age really slowly?"

Bones nodded. "That's my guess." He suddenly got uncomfortable, thinking about other means of old age. Mostly alien.

"What?" Mack asked, noticing his demeanor change.

"There may, or may not, be things in this world, or outside of it, that could aid in something, or someone, living forever."

"Aliens?" Mack asked, laughing.

Bones looked away, returning his attention back to the low flames. He decided to give Mack clues without actually admitting to anything. She was smart enough to do the math.

The last thing he needed was Tam calling him, asking him why he opened his big mouth to a journalist. Mack, if she wanted to, could expose everything they've tried to hide. Most of what they buried was to keep it out of the hands of people that would wield it nefariously.

Could these creatures' venom be used in that way? Could ScanoGen get a hold of it and weaponize it? It would be just like Norway all over again. He'd need to contact Tam when this was over and have her look into it. She still had her people looking after the discovery in

Norway. If something similar was found here, she'd want to know about it.

He squinted, thinking. Speaking of venom…

"Do me a favor and check on my wound, will ya?"

Nodding, Mack stood. "Turn around so I can use the firelight."

Staying seated, Bones did as he was told and faced away from the fire. Then, carefully, Mack pulled the collar of his shirt away and gently peeled back the layer of dressings.

"Oh, my god." That wasn't what Bones wanted to hear. "The skin around the cuts… It looks like it's—"

Click.

"It has begun."

Both Bones and Mack whirled around and found Dudu leveling his AK47 at them. At the angle he was sitting, Bones' gun was out of sight holstered on his right thigh. If he was slow enough, he might be able to draw it and fire from the hip before Dudu got a shot off. Bones trusted his own proficiency with a gun over Dudu's, even if the situation currently favored the other man.

"Easy, bro," Bones said, holding up his left hand, palm out. "I'm still me. We can figure this out before anyone else gets hurt."

Dudu's eyes looked demonic as the firelight danced within them. He was losing it, that was for sure. Bones needed to convince the guy to drop the rifle before both he and Mack got hurt…or worse.

"Please," Mack pleaded, stepping in front of Bones, "don't do this. He's fine. There is only some minor swelling and a small amount of fluid seeping from the wound. It needs to be cleaned before it gets infected. I was about to tell him that they looked to be healing just fine."

"Liar!" Dudu was about to break. "He is already dead!"

Bones wasn't sure what he'd do. If what Mack said about his injury was true, then he was fine. Dudu, on the other hand, wasn't okay.

"Then, I'll take care of it if he turns."

Shocked, Bones snapped his attention back up to Mack. "You'll what now?"

She glanced down at him, turned her face a little, and winked. "I said I'll shoot you if you get out of hand."

Bones hid his smile. Mack had no intention of doing anything of the sort. Mack's half-smile also said that her assessment of Bones' wound was accurate. He really was okay. Dudu's rifle dipped a hair in response, and then, it altogether dropped, but not from his hands. He looked at them both and then stormed off, disappearing into the shadows surrounding their campsite.

"He'll cool down," Mack said, helping Bones to his feet.

"He'd better," Bones replied, rolling his shoulder again.

"Or you'll do what?" Mack said, smirking.

"I'll kill his crazy ass." Mack's mouth hung open. "I won't enjoy it, but I will." Bones stepped away but stopped. "You know, like fruitcake. I'll eat it if I'm hungry enough, but I won't enjoy it." He shivered. "Ugh…fruitcake. More like grosscake, am I right?"

Mack's mouth stayed agape until someone screamed from out in the darkness. Then, like his butt was burning, Dudu came running toward them. Unsure of the guy's mental state, Bones drew his Taurus pistol and pointed it his way, leveling it his chest as he moved. But as the local got closer, Bones saw that he had a look of terror on his face, not one of insanity.

9

Dudu made a beeline for Bones and Mack, leaping over the flames just as something big slid out of the trees. It wasn't as large as the other one, but this golden snake was still plenty big. It was the size of an average anaconda, but it moved with the supernatural speed its giant-sized relative did.

Landing hard, Dudu plowed into Bones and Mack. Luckily, Bones braced himself and easily halted the man's forward progress. Plus, even injured as he was, Bones was a lot stronger than Dudu, having a foot in height and a hundred pounds on him. Bones grabbed his shirt and one of his arms and literally yanked him to a stop, causing Dudu's feet to leave the ground as he did.

A high-pitch grinding noise greeted them as the hybrid anaconda lifted its front end up, and opened its mouth. Its head stopped ten feet off the ground, its line of sight clearing the flames just fine. Yellow, firelit eyes bore holes into each member of the team as it took them in.

"Keep the fire in between you and it," Bones whispered, studying the creature.

Like the Sachamama, this one also had a feathered appearance, having similar spines running down the length of its body. Its head was the same elongated shape as well. It was plain to see that the smaller one was Goldi's baby. It also confirmed that the creatures did, in fact, reproduce. How old this one was was impossible to know. Even at its more diminutive size, the juvenile "earth mother" could've still been decades old—centuries even.

If they age as slow as we think they do, Bones thought.

Bones fired a shot, but the snake skillfully dodged it, swaying down and to the right. Bones was hoping Dudu would use his rifle, but the weapon was missing, and his arm was bleeding badly. Unlike Bones, Dudu was probably infected with the venom of the Sachamama. He'd be a mindless slave in no time if they didn't figure something out.

"Forget the guns, it's too damn fast!" Bones shouted, holstering his gun and unsheathing his machete. Mack and Dudu likewise pulled free their machetes. "Chop its freaking head off!" Bones took two steps and soared through the air, clearing the low fire with ease.

The quickest way to your destination is a straight line.

Swinging midair, Bones barely missed the creature's face by inches. It slinked back, hissing like mad, fangs showing, dripping with poison. Anacondas didn't usually have fangs—or venom. They, like other constrictors, had sharp teeth, yes, but they were really only used to grab their victims. Then, they'd use their powerfully built bodies to coil around their prey and squeeze.

The golden Sachamama had the best of all the species. Plus, the way it moved told Bones that its muscle mass must've been off-the-charts strong. It could probably crush him to a pulp if it got ahold of him.

Just like mama snake did to the building back in Love—

The backend of the snake whipped around incredibly fast, wrapped around Bones' leg, and lifted him off the ground like he weighed nothing. Bones grunted as his hip joint threatened to dislocate, protesting against the sudden and violent jerking motion. It was an impressive move, albeit, horrible to be on the other end. Now upside down, and defenseless, Bones waited for it to strike.

But it didn't.

Mack and Dudu, however, did.

Busy with Bones, the snake didn't notice the other two humans coming in, hacking and slashing with their bladed weapons. Both made solid contact, digging into the serpent's skin. Each successful strike got a shrill cry of pain out of it, as well as a pissed off, grating hiss. Reacting to the new threats, it dropped Bones on his head, causing him to accordion in on himself, knees to chest. He tried to roll out of the brutal landing but failed miserably. Instead, he floundered like a fish out of water.

"Son of a bi—"

Slow to get up, the snake advanced on Bones' teammates, slinking over him as if he were a downed tree trunk. The feeling gave Bones the willies. It was a sensation he had never felt before, and one he hoped to never experience again. He usually felt no ill will towards the species, but when one the size of an ana-freaking-conda slithered over your chest and face… Let's just say, it quickly changed his mind about the creatures.

"Snakes," he mumbled, "why did it have to be—?"

Bones gagged, trying to wipe the "snake stink" away. But it was all in vain, and it's all he could smell now. Even the charred wood from the fire now only feet away from his face was invisible against the stench. He gagged again, dry heaving as a result.

The shouts of his comrades and raspy hiss of their would-be killer, broke him from it, though. He flipped over onto his stomach, pushed off the ground and stood— only to be tail-whipped and thrown back through the fire, smashing into, and scattering, the lit logs. Embers exploded into the air, sending the serpent reeling away in abject fright.

On the ground, Bones was forced to do two of the stages of "stop, drop, and roll." He stopped and rolled. With his shirt singed and pockmarked with burn holes, Bones struggled to his feet and balled his fists. He watched as Mack bellowed in rage just as Dudu attacked from the other side. Her machete hit home, slamming right into the side of the snake's skull.

As soon as the weapon struck, the serpent went down, thrashing at the blow. The machete was ripped free from Mack's hands and she, like Bones, was knocked away. Mack landed hard but was otherwise unharmed. She immediately sat up and watched from afar as the animal's chaotic movements quickly died down.

Then, there was nothing.

Bones helped Mack up, and they checked out one another's wounds. Bones had only minor scrapes, amazingly escaping the fire with no burns.

He pounded his chest. "Us Injuns are fireproof."

Mack grinned, but grimaced at the effort, sporting a bloodied lip and a lump on her forehead. After catching each other staring, they immediately broke eye contact and looked for Dudu. He was alive and breathing heavily. The local stalked over to the already dead serpent and hacked at its neck, just below the skull, until they came free of one another.

"We take no chances," he said, staring at the decapitated monster with wild eyes.

Bones actually agreed with Dudu, but he didn't voice any agreement. He wanted no part in adding to the guy's intensifying psychosis. After seeing his mutated cousin kill himself and his place of business destroyed, Bones could understand Dudu being a little distraught—vengeful even. He had lost a family member and his livelihood in a matter of hours.

That's a lot to process.

"Bones," Mack said rounding what was left of the fire, "look…"

He followed her and saw what she did. The snake bled, but it wasn't red.

"Gold blood?" Bones asked.

"That is not normal," Dudu said, calming some.

"No shit, Sherlock." Before Dudu could ask who Sherlock was, Bones waved him off. "Never mind."

Hands on knees, Bones examined the body. "What infected and then mutated these things… It's something completely different than anything I've ever seen." He glanced over at Mack and winked. "And I get around."

His eyes lingered on Mack for a moment, appreciating a member of the opposite sex that could get her hands dirty with gusto. While a little boyish for his liking, even a filthy Mackenzie Moore was striking. She was growing on him more and more.

Bones realized he was staring when Mack raised an eyebrow and crossed her arms. He quickly stood and cleared his throat.

"The, uh, commotion is going to bring attention to our camp." He headed back to his spot around the fire. "I think we should get moving ASAP."

Dudu shook his head. "It is not safe to travel at night. Lots of dangers."

"More dangerous than this?" Mack asked, motioning to the headless, twenty-five-foot-l0ng snake. Then, she quickly added. "Besides its mother, I mean."

Dudu shrugged. "Yes, there are other—more natural—predators we still need to worry about. But no, there is nothing worse than these…" he looked for the word, "abominations."

"Good description," Bones said, packing up his things. "What do you think they are?" He tipped his head toward Mack. "I've heard her thoughts. What about you?"

"Before we leave," Mack said, "let me look at that." She pointed at Dudu's arm.

Dudu shook his head, also gathering his belongings, minus his missing rifle. "Do not bother. If it is as I think, and you can only be infected directly by one of the creatures," his shoulders sagged, "than I am already dead. Bones got lucky… I did not."

"That's not true," Mack countered. "You don't know that for sure."

If it was possible, Dudu's shoulders sagged even lower. "But it is true." He looked over his shoulder and met Bones and Mack's stares. "I have seen it happen before."

"What!" Mack's hand went to her mouth.

Bones tilted his head in confusion but then understood. "That's why you've been acting so crazy, huh?" The pieces quickly fell into place. "You saw what happened to your cousin last year, didn't you?" He clenched his fists and stepped toward Dudu. "You knew about these monsters from the start."

After a few seconds of silence, Dudu replied with a soft, "Yes," he stepped away from an irate Bones who stepped toward him, "but no, I did not know about the creatures. I did not see it actually happen. I only heard it." He explained further. "Business was good, but Hernao had gotten himself into trouble with some out-of-town traders."

Bones shook his head. "That's where the guns came from. Your cousin was dealing in weapons behind your back."

Dudu nodded. "He worked for me and threatened to tell everyone that it was my doing. I would lose everything if he did."

"But you said he wasn't trustworthy," Mack said, remembering as Bones did what Dudu had said earlier. "Why would anyone believe him?"

"It does not matter if it was true or not," Dudu replied. "No one would hire me if they suspect that I trade in guns."

Bones looked at Mack. "Would you have?"

Mack could only shake her head. "Even if it was only a rumor and not fact. I wouldn't have involved myself in it just in case it was true."

"Exactly!" Dudu shouted, tearing up.

"So, you fed Hernao to the wolves, or what?"

"No!" Dudu denied. "We were scouting ahead for Igor, just after he arrived. At the time, he was still looking for his giant anaconda." He took a deep breath. "One night, I saw Hernao pulled into the shadows by something unseen. I tried to track him, but could not. I was scared." His eyes fell. "But then, I thought my troubles were over. People disappeared all the time. It is a fate we have come to know." He closed his eyes. "But I was mistaken."

The wall, Bones thought. The whole town lives in fear.

"Hang on." Bones turned around hands on hips. Something he just heard jogged his memory. "Taken? Like Igor?"

Dudu's sorrowful face brightened a little. "Yes,

exactly like Igor!"

"The Sachamama stole them?" Mack asked. "Is that even possible for a primordial animal to do?"

Bones laughed. "There you go again, questioning the possible." He waved his hands in the air. "None of this is possible, Red, yet here we are."

"And what about him?" Mack asked looking to Dudu.

Bones shrugged. "We hope there's a cure somewhere out there. And speaking of that, where are these things coming from anyway? There has to be a nest or something, right?"

He and Mack turned in unison to Dudu.

Dudu nodded. "There is a place of local legend." He hefted on his pack, careful of his bleeding forearm. "There is a place where no one dares to go. A dangerous place."

"Where?" Bones asked, knowing he wasn't going to like the answer.

"Locals in the area call it the Mother's Womb. It's said to be the birthplace of all the evil within the rainforest...and the world. No one has ventured there and returned. The villages surrounding it forbid that anyone goes there."

Bones exhaled hard. Earth Mother, Water Mother, Mother's Womb. It was evident that this forbidden place was the heart of the Sachamama and/or Yacumama's territory.

"What do we do when we get there?" Mack asked, sounding defeated.

Bones glanced down to the shimmering embers of their fire. He recalled how the Sachamama youngling cowered from the flame. He pounded a meaty fist into his palm.

"You have a lighter?"

Mack glanced over to Dudu before answering Bones, looking unsure. "Yeah," she shrugged, "I always do."

Bones grinned like a child about to get into some more shenanigans. "Then we figure out a way to burn it to the ground," he drew his gun and checked it, releasing the magazine before slamming it back home with extra enthusiasm, "and send these things back to hell."

10

Conveniently for Bones and company, the younger snake seemed to have followed the larger one's switchbacking trail, only diverting to seek them out. The stink was easy to follow too.

With his flashlight in one hand and his Taurus pistol in the other, Bones led them through a series of collapsed trees and tall, trampled grasses. Their feet sloshed through the semi-flooded land as they marched onward at a brisk pace.

He glanced behind him. Brisk for me, anyway.

Bones moved one speed. Full speed. Mack, while tired, was the least injured of them and was actually following along nicely. The more and more Bones was around her, the more he was impressed by her. He really needed to stop doubting her so quickly.

Then, there was Dudu… He was falling behind more and more as the minutes passed. The wound, while pretty nasty, shouldn't have been anything life-threatening. The venom coursing its way through his system was the real danger, not him bleeding out.

Even in the uncomfortable heat and humidity, Dudu was sweating buckets. Bones himself was drenched, as was Mack, but Dudu looked like he had gone swimming with his dead cousin. It was a grim thought, but Bones had been severely desensitized by death over the years. Plus, making light of situations was an easier way to deal with things.

Silently, he held up a closed fist, signaling for Mack

and Dudu to stop. There, behind a cluster of tree trunks and shrubs, they rested. Bones had them moving for three solid hours until now, wanting to use the cover of night to their advantage. From what he could tell, the sun had just started to rise behind them.

At least, he thought it was rising. The canopy above him kept most of the sun's rays from striking the earth. It's why the ground had only a scattering of low growth. Looking at his watch, he saw it was around sunrise, give or take.

Snakes "saw" the world a lot differently than people too, Bones knew that, but he didn't want to give them any more of an advantage than they already had. Plus, there was something about moving at night that gave Bones some added confidence in the situation, no matter how dire it was.

SEALs loved the night and with the direction set by Dudu, Bones then inputting the information into his "spy watch," it made their travel much faster and more efficient. Without a plotted course, they could wander around for days and never find civilization again.

"Five minutes," he whispered.

Dudu nodded, looking awful. "I believe we are close."

"How close?" Bones asked.

Dudu shook his head. No knew where the Mother's Womb was precisely from what Bones could tell. It was a general area of death, not a specific location.

"How do you know anyway?" Mack asked.

"Listen," Dudu replied.

Bones heard it, or rather, he didn't hear it. He didn't hear anything at all.

Like when they found the snakeskin, this part of the

jungle was also eerily silent. In between the two spots, they had heard the sounds of life. Bugs, birds, random animals on foot shaking the brush around them. Now, there was absolutely nothing.

They stood there for a few more minutes before speaking again. Bones drained his second-to-last water bottle, while Mack nibbled on a protein bar. Dudu held himself up on the closest tree, panting for air like an overheating dog.

"What are we gonna see?" Bones asked.

"I am not sure," Dudu replied, blinking hard. "Only the oldest living in Lovely have any knowledge of it. Even they only know stories mostly. The last person to try and find this place died forty years ago. More have tried, none have returned." He rubbed his face hard. "No one from our village, or those around us, have seen or heard anything in decades. Yacumama sightings happen quite often. Whether they are legitimate or not... But Sachamama..."

"Ballpark it for me, dude."

"Ball—"

"Guess," Mack interrupted. "What do you think is there?"

Dudu thought for a moment but nodded. "From what I have heard, a large population of the elders think there is some sort of settlement...full of riches." He made solid eye contact with both Bones and Mack. "Mostly gold."

"A city of gold?" Mack asked, stunned.

"Another one..." Bones' comment came with a faraway look. He and Maddock had found something similar in the American Southwest a while back. This being in South America gave Bones another thought.

"El Dorado?" he asked.

"No," Dudu said, confident, "this is something else—something that no one dares to record or even speak about. There are no legends, no fanciful myths about this place. While supposedly beautiful and full of wealth, it only brings death and despair. The people that live in this region do not talk about it for fear of the evil residing there."

Bones laughed softly. "Sounds like a charming place."

Mack's face lit up. "The coin... Could it have come from this place?"

"I would say so," Dudu replied. "It is said that the creatures are obsessed with gold. I believe it is how they found it in Lovely so easily."

"Must be nice."

Mack and Dudu looked at him.

"What?" He threw his hands up in defense. "All I'm saying is that it must be nice to have a sixth sense dedicated to finding gold." He grinned. "Would make my job a hell of a lot easier."

Mack swallowed the last of her snack, speaking as she did. "Where's the fun...in that?" She shoved the wrapper into a plastic bag and stuffed it all in her backpack. "I thought half of it was for the adventure."

Bones laughed hard. "Only if there's something at the end of the rainbow waiting for you, sure. There's gotta be more than leprechauns and unicorn farts for me to call it a successful mission, Red." He jabbed a thumb at his own chest. "Pot of gold or bust."

"Geez..." Mack said, sneering her nose at him.

"Oh, please. Don't give me that look." He turned towards Mack, facing her fully. "Why are you here again?"

He didn't let her answer. "Exactly! We're capitalists. You didn't come here strictly for the fun of it. You, Mack Moore, came for fame and fortune."

"And why am I here then?" Dudu asked, looking confused.

"Because, A) she paid you to be, and B) that." Bones pointed down at his injured arm. Bones crossed his thick arms. "Unless you want to join your cousin in zombie paradise? I can see a sick kumbaya moment with everyone involved singing It's a Dead World After All."

Even though he didn't understand half of what Bones had just said, it was evident that the statement had sobered up Dudu some. Bones could tell he was replaying Hernao's suicide in his head. It wasn't easy to watch someone you know die, and it would take some time to get over.

Time, we don't have. His eyes shifted back to Dudu's arm. Especially him.

Bones hardly knew the guy, but Dudu didn't deserve to go this way. No one did really. Well, Bones could actually think of a few assholes over the years that did, but even this was pushing it a little. A hellish virus that made you listen to, and worship, a monster from the deep, dark jungle. It was as terrible a "curse" as Bones had ever heard of.

But how?

Alien tech was beginning to overtake his mutation theory. The other palpable explanation would be experimentations. The problem with that was that these creatures had been around for hundreds, maybe thousands, of years. It wasn't something new that suddenly arrived out of nowhere. The Yacumama and Sachamama were definitely not new to the area.

Companies like ScanoGen weren't the culprit here.

A naturally occurring mutation still felt right, though. But Bones' luck was never that good. Something ordinary causing the ginormous snakes was way at the bottom of his usual list. If Vegas had odds on it, "outside sources" causing the anacondas' evolution would be the favorite to bet.

"How can we be so close already?" Mack asked.

Bones' eyebrow lifted, silently asking the same question.

Dudu looked at both of them and took a deep breath. "Lovely is the nearest settlement. We, especially, do not venture into the jungle beyond our borders." Dudu frowned. "Though our wall could not protect us…" He continued. "We use the rivers for everything. It was said that the elders of our village angered the gods by building a village so close to the Mother's Womb. Rumors of Lovely being cursed have circulated throughout the years, but we do not speak of it."

"It would ruin the town forever," Mack said, nodding.

"So, you avoid the Mother's Womb instead of doing something about it?" Bones snorted a laugh. "That's pretty lame, bro."

"What would you have us do?"

Bones held up his gun. "Bring a dozen armed villagers and dump your payload. Eradicate them and save anyone else who's taken and killed—or turned, or whatever!" He holstered his sidearm. "Doing nothing makes you as much to blame as the damn monsters."

"Bones, that's not fair."

His head snapped toward Mack. "Damn right it is! How many lives could've been saved if someone had taken it upon themselves to stop the problem." He faced Dudu. "How many more friends and family have you lost to these golden pricks over the years? It's not like you don't have the firepower."

Dudu's eyes darted away from him.

"Ho-ly crap… I'm right, aren't I? There was someone else?"

"Answer him," Mack added, gritting her teeth. She had an equally shocked expression on her face. But it was also mixed with a sick look. Bones couldn't see his, but it was no doubt the same.

"Yes, I have lost another besides my cousin."

Bones squeezed his fists tight, replaying the meeting with Dudu's mother…only his mother. "Your father…" Dudu's wet eyes looked over to him. Bones didn't need a verbal confirmation from the guy to know that he was right.

Bones crossed his arms and calmed. "How long ago?"

Dudu turned away from them, his shoulders sagging. "Almost thirty years now."

Mack moaned and brought her hands to her head. Bones didn't move an inch. He was about to explode. The creatures had been taking people for at least three decades, most likely more. This just confirmed that they'd been in the area for that long, and there was no way to honestly know how long.

Centuries? Millennia?

"Let's get this over with."

Bones stood and parted the brush. What was on the other side was both fantastic and horrifying. He had no idea they were that close to their destination. Mack and Dudu squeezed in next to Bones and took a look for themselves.

"What the shit?"

Mack took the words right out of Bones' mouth.

11

There was nothing… absolutely nothing. Yes, there was a beautiful shrine of gold in the middle of a large clearing, and behind that was a temple of some kind. It too was made of gold, or it looked like it was constructed of gold, anyhow. But there were no people—or snakes, for that matter. The entire place seemed to be deserted.

Or it's a trap and they know we're here, Bones thought, stepping through the brush.

Off to the side of the golden structures were crudely built homes, from what Bones could see, but they looked dilapidated and unused for years. Most were just piles of rubble, caving in on themselves over time, ruined by the natural elements. Whoever used to call this place home no longer did.

The complex was built in a massive depression in the ground. From the circular shape of the bordering tree line, Bones guessed it formerly belonged to a meteorite landing site before being repurposed. Large trees grew within the grounds, their tops connecting to the trees lining the crater. It hid the buildings from anyone looking for them from above.

Natural camouflage. It was an ingenious way to hide what someone…something…didn't want to be found.

"Very resourceful," Mack said, squatting at the edge of the slope. "I'll be curious to know how it was done." She motioned to the canopy above them.

Bones nodded and kneeled next to her. "And whether the complex was built before or after it was hidden away from the world."

"Growth like this," Dudu added, breathing hard, "would take generations. And the buildings…" His eyes widen. "Who? How?"

Bones stood. "Doesn't matter. We have a job to do." He started down the steep grade. "We can poke around after we kill Goldilocks." He glanced back at Mack and winked. "Maybe get some bountiful booty for our trouble."

Quietly, the three of them climbed down the decline. Bones was itching for something to happen, waiting for a group of snake-men to leap out at them from the shadows. He didn't want it to happen, but the stillness of the grounds was worse than an attack.

Looking up, Bones saw that there was just enough sunlight coming through to light their way. With the early morning sun shining in, he zigged and zagged around the lit parts of the temple grounds. It was a natural way for him to move in situations like this.

Even if the baddies don't use guns. He shook his head. Just their teeth and nails. With that thought, Bones didn't know if they were fighting an evil horde of mutated snake-men, or a family of pissed off housecats. Kind of sounded like the latter.

The shrine was first, looking very Mayan of them. A set of stairs, six in all, encased the circular platform. Bones held out a hand for Mack and Dudu to stay back. Taking the steps two at a time, Bones scaled the landing and stood before the altar. And that's what it indeed was, an altar.

A sacrificial altar.

He had just seen something similar in Cabras. Altars made of gold—but unlike the giants within Sardinia—this one wasn't slathered in dried blood. It was quite the opposite actually.

He slid his hand across the fresh-looking gold, marveling at its design. Each end of the slightly rectangular block ended in a huge statue of a snake. They looked exactly like the creatures on Mack's coin. The serpent's here, like on the coin, were raised up into the air like cobras. It mimicked the behavior of the two they had seen so far.

The snake on the right was a duplicate to its sister on the left. If the Sachamama and Yacumama were different creatures, why were they represented as the same? Bones had a bad feeling about everything so far, this was just adding to his spiking paranoia.

"Bones!" Mack shouted in a whisper, getting his attention. She pointed past the altar shrine to the temple. A single person was walking toward the pyramidal shaped structure. It wasn't quite a step-pyramid, like most of the Mesoamerican cultures built, but it was close.

The unidentifiable person stomped robotically up the incline to whatever was within. They needed to investigate the building and see what was being stashed away inside of it. Maybe they could even learn a little about the people who built this place too. Intelligence gathering wasn't exactly Bones' thing, but he knew they needed to learn more about them for his team to succeed.

Hopefully, find a weakness to exploit.

Everyone had a weakness. Bones' weaknesses were his loyalty to his friends and pretty ladies. Chicks dug him, and he dug them back. It was a mutual digging, really. You might say that Bones was a weakness of theirs as well.

"Let's go," he said, scaling the opposite side of the altar. Mack and Dudu circled around it, meeting him at the bottom.

The lone man entered the top-level temple and disappeared from view. With any luck, there wouldn't be anyone watching, and they'd do the same. But once they made it to the foot of the pyramid, they ran into a problem.

Dudu stopped amid a sudden coughing fit, stumbling as he tried to climb the first step. Bones and Mack helped him sit, keeping him from collapsing in on himself. He was burning up too, looking sick as hell.

"Okay," Bones said, "new plan. Dudu, stay here and keep a lookout for anything suspicious while me and Mack go in and have a look-see."

Mack wanted to argue, but Bones knew she also agreed with leaving Dudu behind. There was no way he'd be able to keep up with them. The poison coursing through his system was acting fast. He needed to rest and take it easy for the trek back to civilization.

If he can make it back.

"Come on," he said, tipping his head to the stairs.

Together, Bones and Mack moved much faster than just seconds earlier. Each held their pistols at the low-ready as they climbed higher and higher, ready for anything. The guns would be drawn until there was a reason to holster them.

Not bloody likely.

Bones estimated the pyramid to be seventy feet in height and roughly the same size at the base. It wasn't the most majestic of structures, and with the limited ceiling to work under, Bones wasn't surprised. Any bigger and the monolith would break through the canopy and announce its golden presence to the world.

Once at the top, Bones cautiously entered the temple first and swept the immediate area for any sign of a threat.

Walking heel-to-toe, he stayed silent as he stalked forward. The temple was one large, square room and lit by small torches attached to various points on the walls. But it wasn't the walls that caught his eye.

It's what was carved into them.

"Pictographs."

The word made Bones jump. He didn't hear Mack follow him in. Taking a second to get his heart rate down, Bones stood silently and looked over the closest relief. The pictures were carved into giant slabs of gold acting as the inside walls of the pyramid temple. The one he inspected now, showed a group of people kneeling around a large circle.

"The crater," Mack said softly.

"Yep." Bones had thought the exact same thing. "It looks like the people that originally found the meteorite revered it as something from the heavens."

"They weren't wrong," Mack said, getting a questioning look from him. "Heavenly bodies, right?"

"Right," he said, scratching his head. "I've seen my share of those too."

"What!" Mack said, looking up at him.

He grinned and winked, making an hourglass figure with his hands. "Boy, I have seen my share…"

She groaned. "Do I need to punch you again?"

Bones smiled again but returned his attention to the beautifully carved displays. The next one showed those same people holding long, "S" shapes over their heads, also before the meteorite. Bones had seen ritualistic ceremonies like this before in his travels.

"Snake worshipers."

Things were beginning to take shape, well, fall into shape, so to speak. The primitive natives of the region adulated snakes long before the rock fell from space. It seemed that the meteorite's arrival had only evolved their practices, not started them.

Then what?

The third pictograph further shed some light on the snake people's culture. It depicted a large serpent of some kind—an anaconda—with a grown man inside of it.

"Ugh," Bones said, sneering. "They sacrificed their own to them. They fed the things people."

"Maybe…" Mack said, her voice quivering a little. "Or maybe they only fed them their dead—like a burial ritual?"

Bones raised an eyebrow and looked at her. "And some cultures cut the hearts out of their enemies while still alive."

"Think it was an enemy then?"

He shrugged. "Does it matter. It's pretty damn freaky either way you slice it."

Mack held out a hand to pause the conversation. "So…this lost culture worshiped snakes all along, and then what, became psycho extremists after a rock fell from the stars? Really? That's what we're going with?"

"Well," Bones replied, thinking as he spoke, "I guess that depends on the rock."

"What does that mean?"

"Check it out." He pointed to the next engraving, feeling his stomach drop.

Number four really brought everything full circle. The art wasn't as elegant either. It was almost as if the artist got lazy, or if Bones had to guess, and after witnessing the drone-like behavior of the snake-men, he thought it was a good guess that the minds of the worshipers were devolving—breaking down.

The pictograph showed another snake with a manwich inside, only instead of the person just being fed to the creature, they laid the anaconda on top of the stone. Bones thought back to Goldilock's behavior in Lovely. It studied them, decided what course of action it was going to take before doing it.

"Hmmm."

"What is it?" Mack asked.

"My guess?" She nodded. "Well, and you'll have to just go with me on this… If I had to write a thesis on it, I'd say that the space rock emitted a type of energy and altered the minds of the people here. Then, once that person was fed to the snake and then laid on the rock like our picture here tells us…" He blew out a long breath. "I think the creatures—the Sachamama—somehow gained some of the human's intelligence within it." He looked at her. "Whether on purpose or by accident, they created their own god by combining snake and man and an unknown power source."

Mack was about to laugh but paused when she saw Bones' face. He was serious. He didn't try to explain the things that he had seen over the years. All he knew is that crap like this really did exist. How or why wasn't his department. This, more than most, was a long shot, but it did explain Goldi's intelligence.

"It planned its attack on Lovely—on Igor," he added. "It took its time and attacked at the right time, in the right place." He thought back to the attack, reciting what happened while ticking the decisive moments off on his fingers. "It paused at the wall, a gate it knew it could handle and looked over the village. It chased us back into the building, destroying part of it to trap us. Then, while it went after Igor and the coin, it sent the goon squad in to take care of us."

Mack laughed, but not like when you react to humor. She laughed in disbelief, holding her head as she did.

"Um," Bones said, reaching a hand out, placing it on her shoulder, "you still with me, Red?" She batted his hand away and swung at his face. Bones snagged her closed fist his hand and waited, not letting go. "Is that a yes?"

"Yes, I'm still here… And I hate that name!"

He grinned and released her, turning back to the pictograph.

"The only real question left is, what the hell is that rock?"

12

Before they descended the corkscrewing staircase at the center of the temple, Bones ignited a small red-filtered flashlight. The soft color wouldn't ruin his night-adjusted eyes. Even with the sun coming up, it wasn't bright enough inside the temple grounds to matter.

The breadth of the steps drew Bones' attention the most. They looked just wide enough, and the ceiling just tall enough, for their friend to slither its way down too. Both he and Mack would be royally screwed if they ran into it on its way back up.

"How long did it take them to build this place?" Mack asked quietly. They needed to speak in hushed tones until they knew for sure that they were alone. So far, they had only seen that one person. *If Goldi has been around as long as Bones thinks it has, then there should've been a slew of them.*

"No idea, hundreds of years?" he replied. "My best guess is that as the know-how of the people being captured increased, so did the intelligence of the creature. That knowledge would then be handed down to the humans it controls. While powerful, and creepy, the snake still has its physical limitations."

"Why a temple, though?"

That was a good one. Unfortunately, Bones knew how the minds of men worked. Some wanted their names written in the record books like they were making up for some kind of shortcoming emotionally. Some wanted an overpriced sports car, making up for another type of shortcoming.

"Ego?" he asked back.

"Ego?" Mack replied.

"Yep. The human side of Goldilocks wanted a monument built in its honor."

"And the snake side?"

Bones shrugged. "Not sure. Maybe it's just really hungry."

"Speaking of that…" Mack said, stopping mid-step.

Bones paused his descent too, turning around to face her. "What?"

"If this thing is so old, why hasn't it left and found a more populated place to sway?"

"Well, uh…" Bones had no idea. "Huh, that's a good one." He tilted his head down the stairs. "Let's go ask."

The stairs ended at what Bones figured was five stories or around fifty feet. Whatever created the impact crater, it buried itself deep. Not entirely in tune with geology, Bones wasn't entirely sure if the swampy makeup of the rainforest had anything to do with that. Either way, there was clearly an undiscovered cave system down here that now acted as a meeting place of sorts.

Like the pictographs showed, the people here revered the rock. Is that what was happening now? Were the snake-men worshiping the rock as well as their serpentine god?

GODilocks? He stopped.

Mack ran into him.

"Is that it?" he whispered to himself.

"Is that what?"

He faced her again. "The rock… It's obvious that it's the source of the genetic mutations."

"Duh."

"Stay with me, Red." She balled her fist but refrained from swinging at him. "I think they worship the rock because it brought them their god. They thought it was a vessel of some kind."

"And when the changes started happening…"

"Bingo."

"So, they didn't actually worship the snakes like the pictures showed?"

He shook his head. "I didn't say that." He took a moment to gather his thoughts. "What if the surrounding culture fell into hardship and they prayed to the heavens with their serpents in hand like they always did. Then, one day, poof, our rock falls, and the villagers get their true god."

The only flaw in his hypothesis is that…where did the natives develop the ingenuity to build such a temple? It was molded into the same argument that scientists still debated about the other wonders of the world. Bones figured it was aliens, but he was more of a believer in things of that nature than most.

For obvious reasons.

While alien in origin, the meteorite wasn't technically alien in the form of a super-advanced technology. It was alien because it didn't come from Earth. A heavenly body, as Mack put it. Calling it heavenly was pushing it, though. This was more like something from hell. It was evil in every sense of the word.

"Remember one thing," she gave him a stern look and raised a fist, "Ms. Moore… When people don't understand something, they tend to chalk it up to some kind of divine intervention. Science was once viewed as demonic in nature, or magic because the people of the time didn't know what else to call it."

"What do you call a space rock that turns people into snake-zombies?"

His face soured. "I call that bad news."

They continued down in silence, coming up to a landing some feet later. It led them… Bones didn't know. He looked at his watch to confirm their location via satellite, but only got a blank screen and a red light. They were too deep to correctly link up.

Off the grid.

Gun forward, Bones steadily moved on, using his expertise in the wild. Mack's athletic frame and a keen sense of awareness allowed her to do the same. Unless it was Maddock by his side, Bones usually had to support more than himself in a fight. So far, he had yet to jump in and rescue the "damsel in distress." He honestly didn't want to embarrass Mack either. She was a proud person, and Bones respected the hell out of that. So was Bones, for that matter. He was just more vocal about being awesome than most.

The large, but dull, corridor ended a hundred paces later. Bones had, apparently, been subconsciously counting his steps. When they neared the end, he saw something he dreaded in his flashlight's red-tinted aura.

There was another staircase that went deeper.

"Freaking wonderful."

Mack felt his pain but vocalized it with a series of curses and growls. This one headed down and to their left.

"Well, then," he said, starting off, "down we go."

"Again…"

Bones smiled. Mack was definitely growing on him.

Like the spiraling staircase above them and the corridor too, these stairs were also somewhat unremarkable. He didn't notice it before, but the steps themselves were well worn. It reminded him of how water could erode rock if given enough time.

The image of Goldilocks slithering up and down the stairs flashed across his mind. The beast used this path regularly, he was sure of it. Its girth could easily do the job. If they weren't careful, he and Mack could literally walk into the "belly of the beast."

"These are different," Mack said, noticing something Bones didn't.

"How's that?" he whispered back.

"This staircase is more of a banking arch, where the other set was a tight spiral."

She's right, he thought. The construction of the steps was unquestionably different than the set they had just descended. To their left, through packed stone and earth, must've been an enormous chamber of some kind. Reaching out, he slid his bare hand across the wall and stopped.

"Strange…"

He paused and took a closer look. Lifting his light, he showed the hellish glow on the left-hand wall and was confused by what he saw.

"That's not what I expected."

"Nope," Mack agreed. "Look at your hair."

"I can't, it's on my head."

Mack rolled her eyes, touching the wall as well. Bones was astonished to see her hair lift like it had been hit with a charge of static electricity. Feeling the back of his head, he finally found his long ponytail floating like her own was.

The wall itself was made of compacted soil, pieces of wood, rotten detritus, and chunks of naturally formed stone. And apparently, it held an electrical charge. Huh.

Looking up, he saw something different, however. The ceiling above, the wall to their right, and the stairs themselves were, in fact, stone.

"Why is one wall not stone?" Mack asked hands on hips. She had let go almost immediately after touching the wall.

"What the hell is this place?" Bones asked aloud, knowing he'd get no answer. He pulled his hand away, feeling a slight tingling sensation in his fingers.

They stood still in the mild dankness. There were so many unanswerable questions that it was making Bones' head spin. Usually, there was an explanation and an answer, then a fight of some kind. So far, it had been a lot of random-ass events jumbled together into a crappy stew of crap.

It meant that there was something substantial on the other side holding up the natural earth to form a wall. Bones needed to see it—the unknown anomaly. He had to know what it was. So, he moved off quickly, leaving Mack scrambling to catch up. He knew she would, though.

The stairs ended moments later, revealing an opening ahead, and it was lit from within. The light rolled like it was made of water, looking like there was a monster-sized lava lamp shining from within.

"It's gold," Mack announced, looking stunned.

"Um, duh?"

Bones wasn't sure why Mack was surprised. Then again, he could guarantee that she had never seen anything like this before. Weird colored light was just a walk in the park for Bones and his team back home. If Mack was shocked by something as simple as a funky light, then she'd probably fall down when they saw what was on the other side.

Then again, I might too.

With practiced caution, Bones crept forward, laying himself flat against the inside of the doorway. Mack did the same on the right-hand side. Facing away from the light, they took a second to collect themselves, readied their weapons, and…an easily identifiable grinding sound reverberated around them, shaking Bones' teeth. It was the loudest he had heard Goldi since first laying eyes on the monster.

Why does it sound bigger?

Closing his eyes, he gritted his teeth and glanced at Mack. She nodded to him, telling him she was ready when he was. Nodding back, Bones mouthed a countdown from three to one. On one, they both spun out into the opening and took in—

"Damn…"

Before them was a cavern of light. It was honestly hard for him to see anything. It was only in between golden undulations that Bones could see their foe. Goldilocks was fifty feet below them, in a second crater. The serpent was wrapped around a splintered, black stone. Seeping through the cracks in the rock was a molten material. It was the color of liquid gold.

"The source."

Goldilocks was coiled around the rock, squeezing it tightly, cracking it further. With every new snap of stone, the meteorite glowed brighter. With the added illumination, the giant Sachamama also glowed brighter.

Its head was high in the air, directly above the top of the rock. If it were to turn around, it would immediately spot Bones and Mack. They were eye level with it and would easy pickings.

He glanced at the surrounding area, at the base of the

rock, and found hundreds of snake-men…and women. It was the first time he had seen a member of the opposite sex in the mutated form.

Snake-chicks.

The worshipers were standing on mounds of treasure too. Everything from gold to silver to precious gems were present. It was the vast wealth that the local legends said would be here. It also explained why the creature never left. It loved its treasure trove too much to abandon it.

And mixed within the booty were giant-sized bones. From the shape and length of the corpses, "Bones" knew he was looking at the remains of several oversized snakes.

Good god… Well, that explains the second snake on the coin.

It confirmed that there was once more than one of the creatures roaming the region around the temple. The smaller serpent's existence made perfect sense now. It was definitely Goldi's young, and from the number of skeletons in front of him, Bones figured there had been many over the years.

Goldi squeezed again, causing the stone to crack once more. When it did, the creature began to sway slightly, revealing a prone form laying on the rock. Form their vantage point, they could see who it was very clearly.

"Igor."

Bones wasn't sure if the guy was alive or not. The fact that he was there at all proved Dudu's "taken" theory to be true. But what of the others? Goldi didn't consume all of the people it took, that was for certain. In Igor's case, the thing brought him here to…do what exactly?

Mack stepped forward, seeing Igor too. Bones grabbed her arm and shook his head when she looked up at him. He didn't meet her gaze, though. Instead, he saw her face him in his periphery, too busy with the display of "alien" power to do so.

Bones and Mack witnessed Igor's purpose for being there moments later when the Russian shrieked in agony. His arms and legs shot out to the sides, and his body rose off the rock, levitating on an invisible cloud of pure energy. Then, like Alan Parrish in Jumanji, his entire body broke apart, turning into dust, all of which rose into the air, right into the serpent's open maw.

"Are you…" Bones didn't know what to say. "It disintegrated him." He met Mack's stare this time. "It consumed his essence—his very being." His eyes darted back to the creature. "That's how it gains its knowledge. In this case, it wanted Igor's expertise on snakes. The rock's energy must prepare Goldi's prey for the conversion. It eats their freaking souls and—"

Goldilocks was looking right at them. Bones could've sworn that it smiled at them like they were two bowls of piping-hot porridge.

He shoved Mack back the way they had come. "Run."

13

A buttload of stuff happened all at once. Bones unloaded his entire clip, not into Goldilocks, but into the already fracturing meteorite. If the space rock was the creature's source of power, then Bones needed to destroy it. He'd then deal with the golden prick's wrath anyway he had to.

Every single shot found its mark. Bones was a damn good shot. The final bullet did the trick too. It shattered a large section of the black stone, causing a wave of energy to lance out and cut down half of the snake-people gathered around it. But unlike Igor, the mutated worshipers turned into solid gold statues not particles of golden dust.

Holy crap!

Unfortunately, the accidental weapon didn't have the same effect on Goldi. Yes, it shrieked, but it wasn't in pain. It honestly looked like the monster was enjoying the influx of gilded power as it entered the snake's body.

"Well, damn," Bones said, watching Goldi grow before his eyes. He turned and saw that Mack had taken his advice and ran for it. Whether she knew he didn't follow or not, Bones wasn't sure. If she was smart, and she was, Mack would try to save her own ass instead of helping him here.

Another wave of energy passed over Bones' head, and he had to dive to the ground to avoid the same lethal result as the people below. Then, the cave walls flexed and shook, expanding outward. The pressure building from the now vibrating meteorite was causing the place to deteriorate as the seconds passed. The energy seemed to only affect the living too. The dome around him didn't turn to gold. Watching from the landing above, he peered back beneath his perch and watched Goldi's form swell again.

Is it going to pop? Bones asked himself. Maybe an overload or something? And why isn't it turning to gold? Shit!

Twin arching beams of swirling gold swiped through the cave again, solidifying the remaining snake-people into lifeless statues.

The energy was, for some reason, being successfully absorbed into the glowing, now 150ft long, feathered anaconda. As it grew, it started looking more and more like the Mesoamerican version of the creature. It was changing into what he'd describe as a wingless dragon. Black accents formed atop its skin as well, appearing as a beautifully chaotic pattern down his back and across the crown of its enormous head.

His perch cracked directly beneath him, causing the still prone Bones to crabwalk backward as the landing gave. He practically dove for the stairs as the rest of the platform fell away beneath his lower half.

There, dangling over nothing, Bones scrambled for purchase, and just as his sweaty hands were about to slip, his foot found a small outcrop of rock. He shoved up as hard as he could and got a knee up. From there, he pulled himself up and hauled ass back toward the surface.

As he ran, the inner wall, now to his right, began to shake apart. Blinding light blasted through holes as he moved. Each one stumbled him some, making him squint and navigate the worn, upward grade with his eyes practically shut. Just like the right-hand wall, the steps themselves cracked and buckled.

Twisting his ankle and falling flat on his face, Bones tried to stand but was sent to the floor again when the earth around him quaked. He growled against the sharp pain in his lower leg, dug down deep, and pushed it aside. Concentrating on the task at hand—his escape—he stood and limped forward, using the still intact left-hand wall as a brace. So far, he had yet to see anything from Goldilocks, though he could still hear it shrieking somewhere behind him.

Bones cursed his usual bad luck. He hoped the creature was back there dying, but, unfortunately, he knew better. Knowing him, it was probably getting bigger and bigger with every successive blast of energy.

Blowing up the meteorite and overloading the power flowing into the giant serpent was the only plan Bones could come up with at the time. Acting instinctually, he did what he needed to do. He rarely second-guessed himself, but Bones was beginning to think that what he did was wrong.

The area behind him was decimated by a freight train of gold when Goldi smashed through the weakening natural-earth divider. Slamming into the adjacent wall, the impact seemed to stun the behemoth, giving Bones time to regroup and flee. Regrettably, he slipped and sent a small clattering of pebbles back the way he had come.

The creature took notice.

"Crap," he said, witnessing its enormous, vertical slit of an eye shift towards him. Its head being so large told Bones that the thing was at least d0uble its original size already. So far, his plan had failed, only making the creature bigger and stronger.

During a momentary lapse in quakes, Bones, despite

his throbbing ankle, ran up the steps, slinging profanities the entire way. He dodged man-sized boulders as they came rolling down the extra-wide staircase, doing the same to projectiles thrown from the collapsing natural wall.

He could already see that the section ahead of him was missing. In less than a heartbeat, he'd have an open window to the chaos below. About to make his climb while peeking right, Bones paused his continued ascent when the stairs folded in on themselves. The only thing left was a sliver attached to the left-hand wall.

"Freaking awesome, dude."

Laying his back flat against the stone, he shimmied across the open void. As he did, he was, indeed, given a front row seat to the unearthly destruction of the space rock's final resting place.

The rock itself was gone—replaced by a column of molten, swirling energy. It was the same stuff he had seen earlier when Goldi voluntarily cracked it. The outer shell, the black rock, must've kept the alien power from going supernova.

Like it is now.

"Whoops. My bad."

Even if his "blow up the source of the monster's power" plan worked as he wanted it to, who knew how much of the rainforest surrounding the temple grounds would go up in flames. This thing could be a nuclear bomb's level of destruction, killing every living thing around it.

Including Bones.

And Mack.

And Dudu, if the guy was still alive.

"Double whoops."

Halfway across the precipice, Goldi slid into view. Now, more than ever, the Sachamama of legend resembled an ancient dragon of the region's folklore. Even more of the feathered spines could be seen growing above its eyes. Even the mohawk running down its back looked more like a regal mane of hair. It was a cross between the Maya's version and what you'd find in the Chinese culture.

Thankfully, Goldi didn't sprout a set of wings or any legs. It was still a serpent in form…just really, really big. With nowhere to go, Bones was SOL when it turned on him and lunged forward. Opening it enormous fanged mouth, it unhinged its jaws and…missed.

Eyes closed, Bones had waited for death's cold fingers to finally wrap around his busted ankle and drag him to hell. Instead, Goldi's upper and lower jaws hit the rock and got wedged open. Bones was inside the creature's mouth, but still standing on the tiny ledge of stone he was before. Calmly, but quickly, Bones expelled the empty mag from his Taurus pistol, slapped in a new one, aimed the barrel down its throat. He squeezed the trigger three times.

The serpent's reaction was instantaneous. If it had shaken its head side to side, one of the four-foot-long fangs would've cut him in half. But, like most living things when suddenly hurt, Goldi reared back, away from Bones. He dove left and scrambled up the tunnel, putting as much distance between him and the ridiculously terrifying monster as he could.

Goldilocks roared in unbridled rage. It was a sound that Bones had heard from multiple species over the years. It was an unmistakable sound, one mixed with both anger and frustration. Goldi had overshot its mark—Bones—

and failed to end his life, something he was appreciative of. But, like most cunning adversaries, it wouldn't miss again. Next time it had the chance to kill Bones, it would.

The hallway to the spiraling stairs seemed mostly intact, until the floor behind him came apart, spreading towards him. Bones ran at full speed, gritting his teeth against the agony of his mangled ankle. It wasn't broken, though, he knew that much. If it had been, Bones would've already been long dead. It was closer to the injury someone would receive shooting hoops, a classic "rolled ankle."

The next set of stairs came quickly—and so did the advancing cracks in the ground. They practically followed him up the twisting incline, but at a much slower pace. It was obvious that the higher he climbed, the further away from the epicenter of the quakes he was. He was so transfixed by the world around him that Bones forgot to look at the world in front of him.

Not having another upward step to take, he tumbled forward, taking most of the fall on his chest and face. It was the only time he was thankful for taking a header. It prevented him from further injuring his ankle.

But he nearly broke his right cheekbone instead.

"Ow…" He slowly rolled onto his back and breathed, catching his wind. He poked and prodded the parts of his body he could reach, making sure there weren't any other bumps or bruises he didn't know about. Adrenaline was a funny thing like that. It hid the worst pain in the known universe when pumped hard-enough through the human body.

Bones had experienced the "adrenaline high" many times in life. He knew he was going through one now. What he dreaded, if he survived long enough to dread anything, was the pain he was going to feel when the sensation eventually subsided. The "adrenaline crash" he was going to feel was going to be, in a word, unpleasant.

"Can't wait," he said, gingerly sitting up.

"Bones!"

Flinching, Bones felt something in his lower back pull.

"And so, it, ugh, begins…"

Two hands grabbed his shirt and helped him stand. Mack, blood running down one side of her face, was alive. She looked like hell, but, then again, so did Bones. He felt like it anyways. Even the adrenaline coursing through his system couldn't hide every little nick he had picked up along the way.

"Never," he said, groaning as he stood, "call me again."

She smiled and looked around. "Deal."

Neither one of them wanted to do this for a second time.

The temple walls shook, causing pieces of the priceless pictographs to fall and shatter. Bones frowned at the sight. Even a man of his taste could appreciate them for what they were. Mack pulled on his arm.

"I was going to go check on Dudu, but…"

He saw why she didn't a moment later. The stairs leading back down to the vacant grounds below were a disaster. Some of them had survived the quakes, but most didn't. There was no way for them to climb down without seriously injuring themselves. The ground shook beneath them again, confirming what Bones had feared already.

"We won't make it. We could get thrown from the side and break our necks."

The boom of a large impact made both of them

jump. Bones wheeled around and aimed his gun. Mack did too. But there was nothing to shoot. The only thing there was was a piece of gold the size of a dining room table. It was thinner than he thought it would be, but looked plenty strong enough to—

He ran over, grabbing Mack's arm as he did. Half-dragging her, she must've understood what he wanted and helped him slide it back over to the stairs. It was going to be a crazy ride, but what the hell at this point, why not?

"This is psychotic," Mack said, shaking her head.

"No," Bones said, "staying here a second longer… Now that is psychotic. Go!"

They shoved and leaped onto the dense, flat mattress-style surfboard. Holding onto one another, they rode the gyrating staircase of doom, picking up speed as they did. As they moved, their ride broke apart bit by bit. They instinctively scooched closer together, Mack practically climbing into Bones' lap. There was no deeper meaning other than not wanting to fall off and die.

Not dying would be good.

Behind them, the temple imploded, caving in on itself. They spun and watched it disappear from sight. But as it did, it then shot back into the air along with something else.

"Ittt caaan't beeee," Mack said, her voice fluttering along with the terrain.

"Yeppp, iiit isss," Bones replied.

Goldilocks blew through the temple's remains like it did the side of Dudu's business the day before. After descending and then ascending the building, Bones knew just how solidly built it was. Even if it was falling to pieces, nothing should've been able to shoulder through it like that.

"Whaaat do weee dooo?"

He shrugged. "Wanna scrrrew?"

"Whaaat!"

He was laughing on the inside. "I sssaid...we're screwed."

The last two words came out fine, occurring on level ground. They slid together for a moment, spinning like a top until they hit something. Their ride shattered, throwing Bones to the left while carrying Mack further on ahead.

Feeling like a load of clothes in the dryer, Bones rolled for what seemed like minutes. Finally, he landed on something soft and pliable. It was only until he opened his eyes, and got the room to stop spinning, that he saw Dudu's empty, dead eyes staring back at him.

14

"Gah! Holy—" **Bones'** reaction to seeing Dudu's lifeless form was interrupted by a roar so loud it threatened to pop his eardrums and most of his head too. It was Goldilocks' grinding hiss mixed with the sonic boom of a fighter jet. The combination felt like they were going off right in front of him, not a hundred feet overhead and twice that distance away.

Peeking at Dudu, Bones saw what had happened to the guy. His wound looked like it had done him in. He was dead because of the temple, not the virus. Bones could see that scales had formed on his arm before he passed. It confirmed that the venom was the cause of the mutations. He died before he could turn into a monster.

It's what he would've wanted.

Next, was Mack. She was out cold atop a pile of busted gold. He couldn't see her face from this angle, but he could see that her back was still rising and falling. She was hurt, but alive. Come to think of it, only he and Mack made it out alive.

Dudu was gone.

So was Igor.

As were all the people below.

Then again, the snake-people were already long gone, to begin with. There was no coming back from there—none that they found, anyways. If there was a cure of some kind, it hadn't been discovered yet.

How could it? And in the case of the people within the temple grounds, why would there be one? Why would the creature ever want to fix what was done to its people? Answer: Never.

Leaning out from within the devastated pyramid, Goldi arced its hulking form over Bones. He could only stare in awe at the mighty, golden goliath as it slinked down toward him. He raised his pistol but held his fire, knowing it wouldn't do anything against a being this size.

"Now what?" he asked himself, feeling the earth shake under him. The space rock's energy was still trapped beneath Goldi and was threatening to rip the area apart from the inside out.

"Nothing." Bones stumbled backward. The serpent's eyes narrowed. "You can do nothing."

It was a raspy whisper, and it was in his head. The mammoth in front of Bones... It was talking to him.

"How are you speaking?" Bones asked, gripping his gun harder. Was he changing too?

"The venom in your body, I can sense it. It connects us."

"Great, so I'm basically Harry freaking Potter..." He shook his head in disbelief. "Am I turning into one of your slaves?" He spat the words in anger.

"No, Bones. You were lucky."

"Hang on, Bones?" He looked over to Mack and Dudu. The only way the creature could know his name is if— "Igor?" Goldi grinned a sickly grin, showing him its man-sized fangs. "So, you do gain the intellect of the people you...acquire."

"Only those that I want. I learned long ago that not all humans were worth assimilating. Some were better off as my army."

"The snake-people?"

"Yes."

The rest of the temple collapsed beneath the unyielding girth of the monster before him. Bones backpedaled, grabbing Mack, and dragging her away from the destruction. Even the grounds around the pyramid caved in and fell into the secondary crater.

Turning around, Bones saw the sun shining through the enormous hole in the canopy above. Goldi had punched straight through it, finally revealing this place to the world.

What's left of it, anyway.

If anyone was watching, they'd see a larger-than-life gold, dragon-snake protruding from the treetops like a massive, wriggling piece of, well, gold. The sun's reflection would make it easy to see from every corner of the Amazon. But again, there had to be someone looking in the first place.

Glancing at his watch, Bones was happy to see that he had a strong signal—not that it mattered. Yes, he could send a message, even call someone, but they wouldn't be getting here anytime soon. Maddock, Tam, the Salvation Army… It didn't matter who he contacted.

Bones was on his own.

"And," it said, sneering, "you murdered my young."

Bones cringed. He was hoping Goldi wouldn't bring it up.

The ground dropped beneath his feet, jamming his ankle further, while causing him to lose his grip on a waking, moaning Mack. Then, like a sick carnival ride, the terrain tilted inward, toward the creature. He dove forward, snagged her wrist, and threw away his gun. Next, he unsheathed his replacement combat knife and drove it into the ground. The blade pinged off an unseen stone, and it took two more tries before the blade edge finally bit and held onto the landscape as it increased its tilt.

Flashes of light could be seen from deep within the forming canyon. The plan may have worked after all. The rock was about to go supernova. Hopefully, the surge in energy would kill Goldilocks where it stood. It was a grim thing to think since it would most likely kill him and Mack too.

Mack awoke, kicking and screaming.

"Settle down, Red. I got you!"

She calmed and understood. Spinning around, she dug the tips of her toes into the earth and relieved him of some of her weight. Following his example, she drew her own knife and plunged it into the packed soil.

"Climb higher!" he yelled, getting a nod from below.

Goldi hissed and hollered, responding to something happening directly below it. It was in pain, which stunned Bones. What could hurt something that big?

"Look!" Mack shouted, pointing.

Bones paused his ascent long enough to smile. The base of Goldilocks was slowly turning into a solid mass of gold. The swirling vortex of energy beneath it was too much, even for something as powerful as Goldi. He watched as the thing failed to rip itself free from the rock's embrace, freaking out like anything in its position would. It had seemingly lost interest in the two puny morsels fleeing the scene, more worried about its own survival than anything else.

In between screeches, Bones heard something else in the air. It was a sound he knew all too well. In this case, it was a pleasant one. Somewhere there was a helicopter coming in for a closer look. The wup, wup, wup or rotor blades announced the aircraft's arrival seconds later.

Bones didn't care who was in it. He was just damn

happy to see it. It could even be agents of ScanoGen for all he cared. He'd worry about escaping custody later as long as he and Mack got airborne in time.

Mack.

Looking down, he didn't find her. Did she fall?

"Lose something?"

He snapped his head left and found her even with him. Startled, he almost let go of his knife hilt. Her long frame and lighter build made it easier on her. Plus, she didn't have a busted ankle slowing her down.

The temple grounds settled and bulged slightly, turning the land into a steep set of steppingstone-like protrusions. Bones and Mack abandoned the much slower, terribly straining escape route, and climbed boulder to boulder, mound of dirt and wood, to mound of dirt and wood.

The chopper set down a dozen feet overhead, just outside the zone of destruction. Thankfully, the pilot knew what he was doing and didn't shut down the rotors. If the ground fell out from beneath the craft, he could just yank on the collective and hover in place. Then, the rear door slid open, revealing a face that shouldn't have been there.

"Move your butt, Bones!"

He stopped and cocked an eyebrow. "Tam?"

Then, he saw the pilot. He was actually a she. "Kasey?"

Kasey Kim was a member of the Myrmidon Squad, along with Tam herself. She was attractive, a mixed-blood Korean-American, and a very skilled pilot. Bones had tried several times to advance their working relationship. Kasey rejected him every time.

"Why are you here?" he said, climbing again.

"Good lord, Bones. Really?" Tam was shocked. "That's the first thing you're going to say to me?"

He shrugged as she held out a hand and helped him up. Mack was already climbing into the rear cargo hold.

"We've been tracking your movements since Norway just in case we needed you and couldn't find you!" Tam had to shout to be heard over the whir of the rotors. Together they climbed in just as Kasey lifted them off the crumbling ground. They hovered in mid-air and watched as the gold ate its way higher and higher until BOOM a surge of energy shot skyward, disappearing back from wince it came.

Opening his eyes, Bones witnessed the birth of the largest golden artifact on the planet. Goldilocks, like its underlings, was now made of solid gold, forever a reminder of what power could potentially come from above. Two good men had died down there too. It was something that Bones hated getting used to.

But he was.

Next, he slid on a pair of sound canceling headphones complete with microphone. They made it easier for everyone to converse with one another.

"I just thought of something," Mack said, looking sick to her stomach. "We never found the second snake!"

Bones shrugged. "No idea and I don't really care."

"You don't care?"

He shook his head. "Not even a little.

"What about the people in the surrounding villages?"

Bones was done. "Let them deal with it the way they've been dealing with it for years." He jabbed a thumb into his chest. "We made this happen, Red. We caused this to get out of hand."

"What are you talking about?" Kasey asked from behind Bones.

He turned. "Long story, sweetheart."

Kasey rolled her eyes and faced forward, increasing altitude and speed.

Tam wasn't as easy to silence.

"What happened here—and don't tell me it's a long story."

He shrugged and gave her the skinny on everything that had happened since he arrived the day before. Tam didn't react to a single thing. She had seen some crazy stuff in her lifetime as well.

"You aren't shocked by any of this?" Mack asked her.

Tam laughed. "Not at all." She tilted her chin to Bones. "Especially when he's involved."

"So," Bones said, getting to the point, "about you being here…"

Tam's eyes flicked toward Mack. "We need your expertise on something of a private matter."

Bones grimaced and held up a hand. "Take us back to Lovely first, then we talk shop."

"What's this private matter?" Mack asked.

Neither one said anything.

But Kasey did. "Good luck getting anything out of these two." She laughed. "You're just wasting your breath."

15

Lovely was a disaster, just as they left it. The small village looked mostly deserted from what Bones could tell. He wanted to find Dudu's mother but couldn't. The only thing he could figure is that she had fled with the others. Dudu's dream of rebuilding Lovely was on hold indefinitely.

Standing near the dock, Bones, Mack, Tam, and Kasey all said their goodbyes. Unfortunately for Mack, she wouldn't be getting a ride from Tam and Kasey. There was too much to talk about, and Mack was a liability. Her being a journalist complicated things even more.

"You did good," Bones said, looking out to the water. A boat was waiting for her. Luckily, not everyone had left.

Mack stood beside him as Tam and Kasey headed back to the helicopter. "Thanks. I'd say the same to you, but this is kind of what you do, right?"

He laughed but nodded. "Yup, this is me."

"Some life…"

He shrugged. "It has its good moments too."

"And bad ones."

He sighed. "Too many sometimes."

Turning, he held out his hand, but Mack threw herself into him, tears streaking down her face. It wasn't an embrace of love. It was one of thanks. He wrapped his arms around her, feeling uncomfortable for a moment. He liked Mack, but not in that kind of way. She was a warrior, one that he respected. Like Nico back in Cabras, Bones may have just found another ally he could count on.

But he also had a life to keep under wraps. He didn't need his enemies finding him so easily because of a story getting out.

He made his move and was surprised that she didn't notice what he had done. Moving quickly, he knew she would eventually and he wanted to be airborne before Mack exploded like the space rock did.

Bones climbed into the cargo hold just as Mack felt for her notebook in the back of her jeans. Not finding it, her eyes tore into Bones. He winked and gave her a sly smirk.

"Sorry about this, Red," he shouted, holding up the notebook, "but this one isn't making it into your magazine!" They lifted off. "I hope you understand the predicament I'm in!"

Mack raised a middle finger but stayed silent. She would never forgive him, and that was okay with Bones. He had broken a lot of hearts over the years and pissed off many more. Mack would get over it and so would he.

"So…" He closed the door and looked at Tam.

"Yes, about us being here." She sat forward. "We found something in the eastern US and knew immediately that we needed you in on this one."

He grinned. "What I was going to ask you was, what kind of finder's fee I could get for that thing?" He thumbed out the window, still being able to see something gleaming in the distance.

Tam didn't share in his glee.

"Why me, Tam?"

Her dark eyes got even more serious than usual. "It's ICE… They're active."

"ICE?" Bones yelled, stunned. "The assholes from

New Mexico?"

She nodded. "You'd know better than anyone."

"Norway?"

She shook her head but looked unnerved. "The tomb is still secure, for now. We've had a couple of incidences—not with ICE, though. What we found there…"

ScanoGen. Those bastards!

Bones bit his lip. "Okay, then, ICE… Where are we going now?"

Tam sat back and relaxed. "What do you know about Flatwoods, West Virginia?"

The End

ABOUT THE AUTHOR

David Wood is the USA Today bestselling author of the Dane Maddock Adventures and several other books and series. He also writes fantasy under the pen name David Debord. He's a member of International Thriller Writers and the Horror Writers Association, and also reviews for New York Journal of Books.

Learn more about him and his work at www.davidwoodweb.com or drop by and say hello on Facebook at www.facebook.com/davidwoodbooks.